Some Books by the Same Author

THE 17 GERBILS OF CLASS 4-A
MARIA'S CAVE
DOUG MEETS THE NUTCRACKER
CROSSING THE LINE
THE MYSTERY ON BLEEKER STREET
THE MYSTERY ON LIBERTY STREET
MEAN JAKE AND THE DEVILS

CIRCLE
OF
FIRE

WILLIAM H. HOOKS

CIRCLE OF FIRE

A MARGARET K. MCELDERRY BOOK

Atheneum 1984 New York

Library of Congress Cataloging in Publication Data

Hooks, William H.
Circle of fire.

"A Margaret K. McElderry book."
Summary: Shortly before Christmas, 1936, eleven-year-old Harrison overhears a notorious local bigot planning a Ku Klux Klan raid on a band of Irish tinkers camped nearby and realizes he must do something to prevent it.
[1. Prejudices—Fiction. 2. Ku-Klux Klan—Fiction]
I. Title.
PZ7.H7664Ci [Fic] 82-3982
ISBN 0-689-50241-9 AACR2

Published simultaneously in Canada by
McClelland & Stewart, Ltd.
Composition by American-Stratford Graphic Services, Inc.
Brattleboro, Vermont
Printed and bound by Fairfield Graphics
Fairfield, Pennsylvania
Designed by Felicia Bond
First Printing July 1982
Second Printing June 1983
Third Printing November 1983
Fourth Printing August 1984

For Candy and Jeff

CONTENTS

BLACK WALNUTS

ME AND KITTY FISHER WERE SITTING ON the back porch working on a rabbit box.

"If that door keeps sticking we'll never catch anything," I said to him. "I told you we need some sandpaper to make the door slide down fast and easy."

"Well, since we ain't got no sandpaper, what good it do you told me?" asked Kitty Fisher.

"You big-time hunters ain't gone catch nothing nohow," said Scrap.

Scrap moved closer to inspect our rabbit box.

The corners of her mouth curled down. And her nose twitched like she smelled something nasty inside the box.

"That's the most cobbled-up thing I ever see," she said. "Rate you going, Christmas vacation gonna come and go, and you be all the way into nineteen thirty-seven before that contraption is done."

Scrap laughed at our handiwork, and suddenly the door dropped down and landed on my finger.

"Ouch!" I yelled, thinking all the while that she must have willed that stuck door to move.

Scrap laughed even harder.

"All right, Miss Magnolia, you're asking for it," I threatened.

Magnolia was her real name. But she'd fight you quicker for calling her Magnolia than if you cussed at her.

The goal of Scrap's life was to tag after us and worm her way into everything me and her brother Kitty did. Her ma said Kitty was born before Scrap, but Scrap was older. She was a scrappy little kid and that's why everybody called her Scrap.

"Magnolia, you better move your skinny butt out of our business," I warned.

She picked up the hammer we had been using and I thought for a minute she might be going to threaten me with it and make me take back that "Magnolia." Instead, she grabbed the rabbit-box door. Snatched it right out of the trap and ran over to the steps and started banging it with the hammer.

"Scrap, you quit that," yelled Kitty Fisher. "You gone crazy?"

She kept banging the wooden door like she was trying to really wreck our trap. Then she walked back over to us calm as you please and slipped the door back into the slot. It fell fast and easy. Didn't stick a bit.

She brushed her hands and said, "You don't need no sandpaper. Just bang them rough edges down and it slides like greased lightning."

Me and Kitty Fisher looked at each other and didn't say a word.

Just then Grandma scurried out on the porch carrying a steaming pan of sweet potato pie.

"Fruitcake's just too much trouble," she mumbled, as she eased the hot pan on the cooling rack. "If you're not going to make it right, you might as well not make it at all."

Aunt Het, our colored cook, appeared in the doorway with another hot pan. She rocked her head from side to side and grunted, "Won't seem like Christmas without no fruitcakes."

What in the world did Grandma mean—no fruitcakes?

Before I could ask she said, "It'll be a dog mess without black walnuts."

"Pecans be just as good," mumbled Aunt Het.

"Pecans!" shouted Grandma. "Pecans in fruitcake? That's sacrilege. Pecans got about as much character as hominy grits! If you want something to crunch in a fruitcake, it's got to be black walnuts."

"Well, it appears to me the Lord intended us to use pecans this year," said Aunt Het. "Blight got all the walnuts around here when they was still little hard green balls."

"I believe I know where they's some walnuts," said Kitty Fisher.

Everyone turned to look at him.

"You know very well the blight got 'em all, middle of the summer," reminded Aunt Het.

"They's one old tree in the Back Albert Newground got some walnuts," insisted Kitty Fisher.

"We could go to look," I cried, eager to get fruitcakes back on Grandma's Christmas list.

"Let's go," urged Scrap.

"You young'uns be looking for any excuse to go rambling," said Aunt Het.

"Grandma, if we find some walnuts, will you make the fruitcakes?" I asked.

"Harrison, you boys find some black walnuts and I'll make an extra one you can cut *before* Christmas."

"You got a deal, Grandma," I yelled, jumping off the porch. "Come on, Kitty Fisher, we got walnuts to find!"

Kitty hopped off the porch and we headed for the patch of woods that concealed the old tram road.

As we raced out of the yard, I heard Grandma say to Aunt Het, "Can't refuse my favorite."

Kitty and I were running shoulder to shoulder toward the tram road.

We were racing, but we weren't admitting we were racing. I knew if I pulled one step ahead of Kitty, a real race would be on. Kitty knew it too.

Suddenly something rattled behind us and Scrap zipped right past us shaking a couple of tin buckets.

"Where you think you going?" called Kitty Fisher.

"I'm a hound on the scent of walnuts," she howled.

"We got to let her come," I said to Kitty. "She is the only one remembered to bring the buckets."

"First one to the tram road get to shake the tree," called Scrap. Then she yelled, "Haul ass!"

That's all we needed. Me and Kitty Fisher tore after her. She gave us a good run for it but we were a full year older, our legs were longer, and we soon passed her. Kitty would have won if he hadn't stumbled on a root just before we got to the edge of the woods and the entrance to the tram road.

"First at the tram! I get to shake the tree," I cried.

Standing there panting for breath, I got the feeling that always comes over me when I'm moving on the tram. It's very quiet; there's a hush over this old road like it's been lost for a long time. You feel it the strongest when you're alone. Your feet are light on it. When I jump over a dead branch I feel like I'm floating. Gravity is very weak along the tram.

We walked along without saying anything until we got to the creek that cuts across the tram road. They say there used to be a fine bridge over the creek, but all that's left now is some slimy trestle ties that used to hold up the bridge. It's a place where water moccasins like to sun in the summertime.

"You want to cross one at a time or all together holding hands?" asked Kitty Fisher.

"Let's go together," I said. "I'll go on the middle crosstie and you and Scrap can take the outside ones."

"Eskimo Pie!" squealed Scrap as we started inching our way across the creek holding hands for balance.

Eskimo Pie's an expression Scrap made up a long time ago when Kitty and I first gave in and let her play ball with us. We were gripping the bat with our hands, one after the other, and when we got to the top of the bat Scrap's hand was on the bottom, mine was in the middle, and Kitty's was on top, which made him the winner.

Scrap yelled, "Look, we made a Eskimo Pie!"

We laughed ourselves silly—her brown hand, my white hand, and Kitty's brown hand did look like the chocolate crackers holding the layer of ice cream in an Eskimo Pie. It became our secret. Nobody but the three of us knows what we mean when one of us yells, "Eskimo Pie!"

We were doing fine on the trestle ties until my upper lip started to itch. I knew a sneeze was coming on and I was dying to press my lip to stop it, but here we were stuck together like an Eskimo Pie.

"Ker-choo!" I jiggled so hard I thought we'd all end up in the creek. I'm the kind that always gets two sneezes in a row. "Kerchoo!"

On the second explosion Kitty yelled, "Squat!"

We broke hands and squatted, gripping the crossties to steady ourselves. I ended up straddling my crosstie with my feet hanging down toward the water. Scrap was perched like a bird on hers, trying not to lose her bucket. Kitty got his balance and took the rest of the crosstie at a run. He hopped onto the bank and looked back at us.

"You two gonna ride them bucking crossties over the creek?" he called, laughing at us still trying to get our balance.

Scrap threw the bucket at him. He neatly caught it, turned it upside down and sat on it laughing, while we slid inch by inch along the crossties to the bank.

We chased Kitty down the tram road until it ended abruptly in the clearing where Little Hattie lived. A thin curl of white smoke rose from the chimney of her house. We called it her house but it really belonged to my pa. It had been empty for years when Little Hattie moved in. She had a perfectly good house on a little farm about a mile down the road from us. But one day she walked over and set up housekeeping in the old abandoned house, and that's where she's been as long as I can remember.

"Want to stop at Little Hattie's for a minute?" I asked.

Kitty Fisher and Scrap looked at each other. They didn't answer me.

"Come on, let's stop for a minute," I urged.

"Little Hattie be crazy," said Scrap. "Ma said for us not to fool around her house."

"She is *not* crazy," I argued.

"She talk funny," said Kitty Fisher.

"I don't have a bit of trouble understanding everything she says," I answered.

"She be acting crazy ever since change of life hit her," said Scrap.

"You don't even know what change of life is," I challenged her.

"I do too," said Scrap.

"How can you change life?" asked Kitty Fisher.

"I heard Ma talking about it and it means you

can't have no babies no more. Ma says the baby-making juices dries up and it drive some women plumb crazy."

"You talking junk," said Kitty Fisher.

"No I ain't," argued Scrap. "Ma says it's worse on women that don't have no children, so I figured since Little Hattie never had no babies she must of had a lot of juices to dry up on her. And it drove her crazy."

"That's the weirdest thing I ever heard," I said "I'm going to stop and see Little Hattie."

When we got to the chinaberry tree in her yard I called out, "Little Hattie! You there, Little Hattie?"

Then I saw her plump brown face at the win dow. She motioned for me to come in. Kitty and Scrap sat down on the porch steps.

I walked up to the door. It cracked open about a foot.

"Block in quick," said Little Hattie.

I squeezed in.

"It be a bad day," she said. "Bad omens be blocking around the house."

There was a funny smell in the room.

"What you burning?" I asked, sniffing the air.

"Sulphur and rabbit tobacco," she answered. "Got to block them evil omens out of here."

I didn't like the way Little Hattie was acting. Not like her usual self at all. I had a creepy feeling watching the white and yellow smoke rising in the fireplace. Usually we sat on the porch, and Little Hattie told me stories about the olden days when the tram road had a small track railroad running down it and across the creek. And about the Geeche people who came from South Carolina to work in the lumber camps along the tram road. Sometimes she told me secrets about the grown-ups—colored and white—who lived around here.

She was acting strange today. Maybe Scrap was right about all those juices that dried up.

"Harrison, I had a dream last night. And it was a terrible block. Fire. Fire all around. Fire blocking in from all sides Child, we be blocked in a fiery circle. I seen it sharp and clear. I knowed you be blocking over here today. That dream was a sign. A fiery sign."

I didn't know what to answer.

She laughed and grabbed me under the shoulders and lifted me right off the floor.

"Lift a colt every day from the time he's born, you can lift him when he's a full-growed horse," she cried. "I can still block you off the ground, Harrison."

I felt better. Now she was acting more like my Little Hattie. I wished I could stay awhile, but Kitty and Scrap were waiting in the yard.

"I've got to go," I said. "Kitty Fisher and Scrap are waiting outside. We're looking for black walnuts."

Little Hattie looked worried again.

"A fiery sign," she repeated.

She leaned close to me and whispered, "The best way to block fire is with fire."

"Well, I'd better be blocking on," I said.

She smiled at me, looking like her old self again.

"You're some kind of block, child," she called after me as I slipped out of the fireplace room and closed the door behind me.

I jumped off the porch and struck out for the Back Albert Newground.

"You all coming, or you going to sit there on Little Hattie's steps," I called to Kitty and Scrap.

That started another race and pretty soon we reached the edge of the Back Albert Newground.

"Now where's that walnut tree that managed by some miracle to escape the blight?" I asked Kitty Fisher.

"Right over there," said Kitty, pointing to an enormous old tree standing in the edge of the woods.

We walked over to it. At first sight it looked like Kitty had run us on a wild goose chase. There was no sign of walnuts on the ground. In a good year the ground ought to be covered with walnut shells by December.

Kitty pointed up to the top of the enormous tree. There in the topmost branches were clusters of walnuts, dried in their shells, looking like brown Christmas balls.

"Kitty, you got a sharp eye," I cried.

"Yeah," said Kitty, "but we ain't got 'em yet. Them walnuts is mighty high up in that tree."

"I get to shake it. I was the first one on the tram," I reminded him.

Then I looked at the tree. It was too big around to shinny up. And the bottom limbs were too high to reach.

"Them limbs look little way up there," said Scrap. "Don't you think the skinniest one ought to go up?"

"Good try, Magnolia," I teased. Kitty backed up against the tree and cupped his hands. I stepped into his hands, then scrambled onto his shoulders and grabbed the bottom limb. I'm good at climbing, my feet can find toeholds in the dark.

I was soon straddling the limb and ready to climb up for the prize at the top.

I worked my way up the tree, keeping close to the trunk and moving from limb to limb.

Finally I was even with the first limbs that had walnuts. I looked out over the Back Albert Newground. It felt wonderful, tingly and scary at the same time. I thought for a second I could take a deep breath and lift my arms and float from the tree right out over the field. It's a strong feeling I have when I climb up high. I can feel it shivering up my back. And I play with it and let it ride me. It's delicious. But I hold on tight till it passes, then I'm a little scared.

I glanced down at Kitty Fisher and Scrap. They appeared short and squat when I looked straight down at them.

"You stuck?" said Kitty.

"No!" I shouted. "Stand back. I'm going to shake this limb."

They scooted from under the tree. They know what a hard bop a falling walnut can give you.

I grabbed the fruited limb with both hands and shook it hard. The ground was peppered with walnuts.

"Pick-up time," I yelled to them.

Scrap and Kitty rushed under the tree with their buckets and began plunking in the walnuts.

I moved up the tree. The branches were smaller, but loaded with nuts. I thought I'd try shaking the tree a different way. I'd seen Pa stand on a limb and vibrate it with one foot pounding up and down on the limb. I got in close to where I could hold onto the trunk and stood on a limb.

"Stand back!" I yelled.

Then I began pounding the limb with my foot. The vibrating worked and I could hear the nuts peppering the ground. Then I heard another sound. A crunching sound that cracked and splintered, and I was slipping away from the tree trunk. My feet were shooting out from under me and I felt my stomach drop out of my pants. The limbs were flashing by me like whips against my face. I was falling. And grabbing. And feeling scared with every pore in my body.

Suddenly, I felt something solid in my hands and I gripped it with all my might. It broke my fall with a jolt.

Scrap screamed.

Kitty Fisher shouted, "Holy Jesus, hold on, Harrison!"

I was hanging halfway down the giant tree, clenching the broken limb that stretched downward and held for the moment, dangling from its splintered break. I glanced at the ground. It was a long, sickening drop to where Kitty Fisher and Scrap stood with their mouths open.

Kitty ran to the tree trunk, but it was too big for him to shinny up. Scrap practically flew up on his shoulders and grabbed the low limb I had used.

"Hold on," she panted. "Hold on, I'm coming."

She worked her way up the trunk to where I was hanging.

"Don't wriggle," she cautioned. "Just hold on. If you move that busted limb might split off."

I could hear little snapping noises coming from the limb. I tried not to breathe. Scrap was straddling a limb, inching her way toward me.

I could hear grunting from below.

"I made it. Hold on! I'm coming, too," called Kitty Fisher.

Somehow he was in the tree.

"Kitty, stop," cried Scrap. "Move out right where you are and grab him by his belt. I can reach his hands from up here."

My locked hands on the dangling branch felt dead. I couldn't tell if I was gripping or turning loose. I closed my eyes.

"Now!" shouted Scrap. "Grab and pull!"

I felt myself falling again. The splintered limb pulled loose and dropped.

I can't exactly remember what happened in the next few seconds but I know they somehow had me over a solid limb like a sack of meal. And they were pulling me back to the safety of the big tree trunk.

We slowly and carefully worked our way down to the bottom limb. It was still about eight feet from the ground.

"We got to swing down and drop," said Kitty Fisher. "Let's all go together."

All three of us swung down and Kitty shouted, "Let go!"

We fell to the ground and bumped into each other, laughing and tumbling around. I was trembling and laughing at the same time. I saw a big limb Kitty had leaned against the tree trunk to help him climb up. Scrap's knee was scratched and bright red blood was dribbling down her brown leg.

Tears started running out of my eyes, but I felt

wonderful. I grabbed Kitty's hand and then Scrap's.

"We'll be friends forever," I said, holding their hands.

"Eskimo Pie!" they both shouted together

MR. BUD HIGHSMITH

"BOTH BUCKETS BE FULL UP," ANnounced Scrap. "Enough for your grandma and some for me and Kitty to take home."

"Let's go home by the woods road," I said, not wanting to take chances on crossing the creek with two full buckets of walnuts.

Scrap and Kitty gave me a puzzled look.

"You know we don't like messing around on the woods road," said Kitty.

The woods road divided our land from Mr. Bud

Highsmith's farm, except that it didn't quite follow the legal property lines. In some places Mr. Highsmith claimed the road went over onto his property. There was a long-standing argument about the land on each side of the road.

It was a mess, and I don't know who was right. But me and Scrap and Kitty Fisher always kept a close lookout along the woods road ever since our run-in with Mr. Highsmith. He once caught us picking huckleberries along part of the road he claimed was on his land.

"What you nigger young'uns doing trespassing on my land!" he yelled at Scrap and Kitty Fisher.

"Hand me that basket of stolen berries, boy," he called to Kitty.

Mr. Highsmith's one big scary man. Kitty dropped the basket of huckleberries and ran. Scrap flew behind him. And I was left facing Mr. Bud Highsmith by myself. He still hadn't acted like I was even there. I wanted to run too, but I was madder than I was scared.

I stood there and watched him pour Kitty's berries on the ground and stomp them with his big heavy boots. "Wouldn't eat no berries picked by them stinking hands."

Finally he looked straight at me and said, "All you Hawkinses is the same–nigger lovers!"

That was over a year ago and we have steered pretty clear of the woods road since then.

Kitty and Scrap were still holding back.

"Come on," I urged them, "we're just going to pass right through. We're not going to stop. Anyhow, we could outrun Mr. Highsmith if we had to."

They followed me, but I could tell they were worried. We walked along quietly. The whole "nigger-lover" business was bothering me. I had tried talking to Grandma about it.

"Grandma, why does Mr. Bud Highsmith hate Scrap and Kitty Fisher and call me a 'nigger-lover'?"

"Child, don't let me hear you saying that word," snapped Grandma.

"What word?" I asked.

"That dreadful word poor white trash uses when they mean *colored*. You've been brought up to show respect."

"But Mr. Bud's not poor," I argued.

"Poor in spirit, Harrison," Grandma explained. "There's more ways to be poor than in money."

"Well, it makes me mad when he calls my best friends, Scrap and Kitty Fisher, by names like that."

"Ignore him, child. Ignore him. That's the best way to handle his kind."

Grandma looked at me and sighed. "I do wish you'd find some other friends, too," she said gently.

"What other friends?"

"Harrison, you're already eleven years old, next year you'll be twelve. The age of accountability."

"The age of accountability? What's that, Grandma?"

"Until you're twelve your sins are on your parents. After that you're responsible," she explained

"But we were talking about my best friends. What's this got to do with Scrap and Kitty?"

"You'll be needing new friends, Harrison."

"You mean white friends, don't you, Grandma?"

"Your own kind and your own kin," answered Grandma.

"But Grandma, I know Het George happens to be your best friend, and you can't get more colored than that."

"All right, young man, just hold it there. First of all you'll be saying *Aunt* Het, showing some proper respect for decent older colored people. Het George is a God-fearing decent person. I'll not have you saying anything against Het."

"Grandma, I really don't understand you."

Grandma looked hurt. I know I should have kept my mouth shut, but I had to say, "I'd still rather play with Scrap and Kitty than anybody else."

Grandma turned her head and asked to nobody in particular, "Why does my favorite have to be so stubborn?"

Scrap shoved her bucket into my hands, pulling me away from my thoughts.

"You carry my bucket," said Scrap when we

were a little way down the woods road. "I don't want *old-you-know-who* accusing me of stealing walnuts from his land."

I took Scrap's bucket and looked at the loaded one Kitty was carrying and hoped we didn't run into Mr. Bud Highsmith. With the luck I was having today, I expected to see him around every bend in the road.

At first I didn't pay much attention to the dog we kept hearing bark. It sounded pretty far off. But the sound kept getting closer and closer. I think it came to me and Kitty Fisher at the same time what it was. We stopped and looked at each other. The dog barked very near.

"That's Rogue!" said Kitty. "I'd know that mean bark anywhere. That's Rogue; old man Highsmith's out hunting."

"And he ain't far off," whispered Scrap.

"We'd better get out of here," said Kitty.

"Haul ass!" I cried, thinking, *I'm going to slip up one day and let Grandma catch me saying that.*

We started to run back toward the walnut tree, but it was a wrong move. We ran head on into Mr. Bud Highsmith and Rogue as we dashed around the first bend. He had a big shotgun in his hands.

"Hold on, there!" he shouted.

I could hear Scrap and Kitty panting for breath.

"What you got in them buckets?" he asked.

"Walnuts," I gasped.

"I've told you to stay off my property," said Mr. Bud.

"But we got these walnuts from Pa's land, in the Back Albert—"

He cut me off and motioned to Kitty with his gun.

"Come over here, boy, and let me see what you've been stealing from my land."

I knew Kitty wanted to run. But Mr. Bud had a gun this time.

Kitty took a step toward Mr. Bud and held out his bucket.

Mr. Bud snatched it from his hand and Kitty drew back.

"Walnuts is mighty scarce this year," said Mr. Bud. "There ain't no extras for the likes of you."

"But, Mr. Bud, these walnuts came from—"

He cut me off again.

"You listen to me, Harrison Hawkins, and you listen good. You keep off my property, and if your nigger friends know what's good for them they better not let me catch their black behinds under any walnut trees of mine."

I felt terrible, but I was too scared to talk back at him.

He waved his gun at us and hollered, "Now let me see how fast you can move it out of here. You got ten counts before I sick Rogue on you."

The big dog slinking at Mr. Bud's feet growled.

"One! Two!" shouted Mr. Bud.

We didn't stop to catch our breath until we were near the end of the woods road.

Scrap plopped down on the side of the road.

"Stop, I be getting a catch in my side," she gasped.

"Me too," I admitted.

Kitty and I plunked down beside her. The Bud Highsmith business was strong on our minds. But I knew we wouldn't talk about it. I wouldn't tell Pa about our run-in. And I was sure Scrap and Kitty wouldn't tell anybody either. We keep a lot of things to ourselves. Just like I knew there wouldn't be a word said about me falling in the walnut tree.

"I'll divide my walnuts with you and Scrap," I said to Kitty Fisher.

Kitty shook his head.

"We's lost the taste for walnuts," said Scrap.

We rested for a few minutes without talking.

Then suddenly Kitty Fisher sat up straight and stretched his neck like he was straining to hear. He held up his hand for us to be quiet. Then I heard it too. We quietly stood up and strained to listen. Someone was tramping through the woods just ahead of us.

Had Mr. Bud Highsmith trailed us through the woods?

A branch snapped and the footsteps sounded closer. We froze where we were standing, waiting to see who it was.

GYPSIES

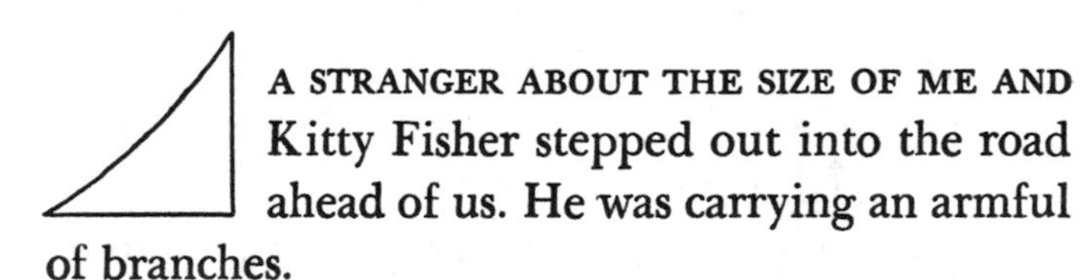

A STRANGER ABOUT THE SIZE OF ME AND Kitty Fisher stepped out into the road ahead of us. He was carrying an armful of branches.

I think we scared him as much as we were scared, thinking he was Mr. Highsmith. He started to run.

"Wait!" I called.

He looked quickly back, then started to run again.

"Wait a minute," I yelled.

He threw the limbs down and really started to run.

"We won't hurt you!" I shouted.

The boy stopped a good distance from us and stood watching. As if he didn't trust us.

"You from around here?" asked Kitty.

He didn't answer, but he didn't run either. We moved a little closer. I could get a better look at him; he was strange-looking. He had real black curly hair, long for a boy. And he wore a cap on his head that hung down in the back and had a red tassel on the end of it. He was dark-complexioned. Even from a distance I could see he had the bluest eyes I'd ever seen.

"It's all right to gather firewood from our farm," I said to him.

He walked cautiously back to the pile of brambles and picked them up.

We moved a little closer.

"Want some walnuts?" I asked, holding out three walnuts in my hand.

The strange boy still didn't say anything.

"Can't you talk?" asked Scrap.

"Aye," said the boy.

"You live around here?" I asked.

"No," he said.

"Well, where are you from?" I asked.

"My family is tinkers," he answered.

"Tinker? I never heard of any Tinkers around here. What's your first name?" I asked.

The boy looked confused. "My first name is Liam. Liam Cafferty."

"I thought you said your last name was Tinker," said Kitty Fisher.

"No," said the boy with a frown. "I said my family was tinkers. Tinkers by trade."

"I bet you be from one of them gypsy families," exclaimed Scrap.

The sharp blue eyes flashed and the boy looked angry. He made a move to leave. Then he stopped and said, "My family is Irish tinkers. Some folks call us gypsies. But my brother says that's because they're ignorant."

I knew the boy was insulting us and part of me bristled, ready for a fight. But at the same time I was afraid he'd run off if we kept questioning him.

"My name's Harrison Hawkins," I said. "And these are my friends Kitty Fisher Shipman and Scrap, his sister."

He nodded his head and started to go again.

"Which way you going?" I asked.

"Down by the creek in that hollow," he said. "My family's camped there."

"Mind if we walk along with you, Liam Cafferty?" I asked. "We're passing by the edge of Broomsage Hollow," I added.

Liam didn't answer. He just started down the woods road with his bundle of dried limbs.

Scrap whispered, "Gypsies always camps by that creek in Broomsage Hollow. But they ain't never come through here in the winter before."

"Just keep quiet and let's follow him and see what's going on," I whispered back to her.

We let Liam stay a good piece ahead of us, but we kept tracking him.

Every time we'd speed up Liam would break into a trot. Then we'd slow down and he'd slow down, always keeping the same distance between us. When somebody does that to me, I can stand it for just so long.

"Let's catch him," I whispered to Kitty and Scrap.

"Haul ass!" cried Scrap.

We started to run. Liam looked back and took off.

He was a fast runner. Even though he was carrying a big bundle of brambles, we couldn't catch him. I heard a dog barking behind us like he was hot on the trail of something. And I heard somebody whistle and then call out, "Where you, Rogue?" It was Mr. Highsmith.

We finally reached Broomsage Hollow and felt safe. The land on the broom sage side of the creek belonged to us. There was no dispute with Mr. Highsmith about that section.

The yellow broom sage stood almost head high in the hollow. In winter it dries, and the hollow looks like a big lake of pale gold straw when the sunlight cuts through it. We didn't see Liam anywhere. He could have been hiding in a clump of broom sage.

"Liam!" I called out.

But there was no answer. A little breeze rustled the golden broom sage.

"Look at that," said Scrap, pointing across Broomsage Hollow toward the catalpa trees along the creek bank.

The place was full of wagons. Gypsy wagons. There must have been about a dozen of them strung out along the creek, nestling under the catalpa trees.

This was the first time I'd ever been close enough to get a good look at the gypsy wagons. In the late summer when they usually passed through, they'd only stay overnight or a couple of days at most. Sometimes I didn't see them at all. Pa would come home one day and say, "Gypsies are camping down by the creek, on their way south." Me and Kitty Fisher sneaked down once but they were already gone, and all we saw was a dead campfire and a lot of wagon ruts and hoofprints. Hanging in one of the catalpa trees there was a cross made with two sticks nailed together. It had a bunch of wilted flowers tied to it. Not knowing whether it was a good luck thing or a bad one, we left it where we found it.

These wagons looked like regular farm wagons with little shacks built onto them. In the back there was a door and some rickety steps. Up front there was a seat like a buckboard for the driver. I figured these must be pretty poor gypsies—their wagons didn't look a bit like the bright-colored ones painted with flowers and signs of the zodiac that I'd seen in storybooks.

"Wow! Take a look at them horses," cried Kitty Fisher.

Down by the edge of the creek some of the gypsy men were watering the most beautiful animals I've ever seen. They were small horses with light brown bodies and yellow tails and manes.

"Palominos, that's what they are," I cried. "I never saw such pretty ones."

Most of the men wore dark pants with bright-colored suspenders and blue shirts. All of them had on caps with little short brims like railroad men wear.

A group of dark-haired women in long dresses was clustered around a fire. There was one woman sitting by herself on the steps of a wagon. Something about her looked different. It was her hair. Her long blonde hair.

Suddenly Liam darted out of the broom sage and ran with his bundle of brambles to the woman with the long blonde hair.

"There he goes," cried Scrap pointing toward Liam.

The blonde woman and Liam spoke for a few

seconds, then walked over to the women gathered around the fire. We were too far away to hear anything, but I was sure from the way Liam was motioning to them and pointing back toward the woods road that he was telling them about meeting us.

The blonde woman called to one of the men who was watering the palominos. He came running over and Liam started talking to him.

"Time to get out of here," said Kitty Fisher.

"You right," said Scrap. "Gypsies steals children and sells them."

"You believe that?" I asked.

"Everybody knows that," argued Scrap.

"Well, I ain't hanging around to find out," said Kitty Fisher.

I wanted to watch a little longer, but I was scared to stay by myself.

THE CROSS

"PA, PA!" I SHOUTED AS WE RACED INTO the back yard. "Pa, there's gypsies down in Broomsage Hollow!"

"The gypsies passed through here months ago," said Pa.

"No, Pa," I cried. "There's a lot of gypsies camped there right now. And we met a boy on the woods road, and his name is Liam, and he said his family was tinkers, and . . ."

"Slow down, Harrison," said Pa. "I believe you. Which side of the Hollow are they camped on?"

"Our side, Pa. There must be almost a dozen wagons."

"Something peculiar about gypsies coming through here this time of year," said Pa. "They ought to be far south of here for the winter."

"Are you gonna go down and see what's up?" I asked. And before Pa could answer, I put in, "Can I go with you?"

Pa said very calmly, "We'll see."

Now Pa loves meeting strangers better than anybody I know. But he's not one to rush into things. Every Bible seller, piano tuner, and peddler that passed our way ended up staying for supper and spending the night. But Pa never invited them right off. They'd get to talking and the time would just melt away. It drove Ma and Grandma crazy because they considered anybody outside the family to be company. And that meant setting up the dining room for a special meal and getting the company bedroom ready for the night. Ma would take turns with Grandma watching Pa and the peddler and watching the clock. If Pa was still talking after four o'clock, they'd nod to each other and start helping Aunt Het get things ready for company.

I'll never forget the time the blind piano tuner came through. He ended up staying two nights because Pa insisted. It was a wonderful two nights when our parlor rang out with the fanciest piano playing I've ever heard. The blind man could play anything you could name or hum. I think we went through the whole *Boardman Hymnal* and the *Golden Book of Favorite Songs.* He won over Ma and Grandma so completely they packed him a lunch when he left. And they insisted I walk with him two miles up the road to Uncle Brodie's house, where there was another piano in bad need of tuning.

I couldn't get that blind piano tuner out of my head for a long time. I'd dream about him tapping his cane along unknown roads, depending on the kindness of strangers he couldn't even see.

Kitty Fisher and Scrap waited by the back steps while I was talking to Pa about the gypsies. I was so excited I clean forgot about the walnuts.

"Grandma!" I yelled. "Come look, we got your walnuts."

Grandma and Aunt Het rushed out on the porch.

"It's a pure miracle," exclaimed Grandma when she saw the bucket brimming with black walnuts. "It's the first miracle in the season of miracles."

Then Grandma came up with an even bigger miracle. She offered Kitty Fisher and Scrap some dinner and a nickel apiece if they'd stay and help me pick out the walnuts. And she gave me a buffalo nickel for my collection. Grandma was generous with old clothes and leftover food, but real money was not one of the things she handed out very often.

We spent a couple of hours beating the brown husks off the walnuts and cracking them with a hatchet. Black walnuts don't give up easily. You have to work for them. Between us we got a quart mason jar full by the middle of the afternoon.

I kept wondering when Pa was going to give in and go down to Broomsage Hollow and check on the gypsies camped there. I knew my pa pretty well and I was sure he couldn't resist. And I was itching to know if he was going to let me go with him.

It was late in the afternoon before Pa whistled for Trixie and Trouble, and I knew he was ready to go. Kitty Fisher and Scrap had already left for home with their nickels.

Trixie came running up at the first call. She's a brindled boxer, and Trouble is her son. But he's brown and white and part bulldog. Pa says they're better farm animals than sheep dogs any day. In a pasture full of pigs you can point to any one and yell, "Catch him, Trixie!" and she'll pick out that very pig and herd him out of the whole bunch. Trouble is trained the same way but he's not as good about picking the right pig.

Trixie gave a yelp and Trouble came running from under the house looking sleepy. Pa still hadn't said I could go, so I came over and started playing with the dogs.

Pa smiled at me and said, "Get a rope for the dogs and tell your ma we'll be back in about an hour."

I ran into the kitchen and told Aunt Het and Grandma to tell Ma that I was going with Pa to Broomsage Hollow and we'd be back before dark.

On the way over, Trouble and Trixie scouted the road ahead of us. I loved walking with Pa and the dogs like this. We didn't usually talk much. We didn't need to, since I thought Pa was about perfect and just being with him was always special. But this was the kind of time when I could talk to Pa if I wanted to.

I wanted to talk to him about the awful way Mr. Highsmith treated Kitty Fisher and Scrap. But I had to think of a way to do it without mentioning their names.

"Pa, why is Mr. Bud Highsmith such a mean man?"

"Well, now, what brought that up? Is there some special reason you're asking?"

"No, nothing special. I was just wondering why he's so mean."

"I'm not denying he's mean, or even that I don't particularly care for him. But I do understand some of his contrariness. He's lived most of his life alone. Never made any real friends around here. Some of his peculiarness comes from pulling into himself like a hermit. And some of his meanness is to keep people from getting too close to him. He's a really scared man."

"A scared man!" I exclaimed. "That's the last thing I'd ever think about Mr. Bud." And I thought to myself, "I don't know if I'll ever be like Pa. He can find something good in just about everything."

When we reached the edge of Broomsage Hollow the dogs stopped and sniffed the air, their short stubby tails standing straight up and trembling.

"Easy, girl," Pa said to Trixie. He knew Trouble wouldn't make a move unless Trixie did first.

Trixie relaxed a moment, looked back at Pa, and went on alert again.

"They've probably got dogs in their camp," said Pa. "Tie the rope to their collars, and hold onto them. I don't want a dog fight before we get introduced."

We crossed the thick broom sage with the dogs choking against their collars.

Near the edge of the camp Pa said, "You wait here with the dogs."

I felt cheated and mad at Trixie and Trouble for holding me back.

Pa walked into the camp and called out. Several men darted from behind one of the wagons; I think they were playing some kind of game. One of them had something like a checkerboard in his hand.

In just a few seconds Pa was shaking hands all round with the men. They were talking but I was too far off to hear. And the wind was blowing their voices toward the creek away from me.

Up close I could see that each wagon had a big wooden water barrel lashed underneath between the front and back wheels. There were hooks around the eaves of the shacks where tin buckets, tools and horse gear dangled. I noticed one wagon that looked bigger than the others. It had a single shaft in front; that meant it was pulled by two horses.

Pa and the men moved over to the big wagon. A huge woman in a billowing flowered skirt, with a fringed shawl around her shoulders, filled up the narrow doorway. She looked more the way I thought gypsies ought to look. The gypsy men did a lot of gesturing with their arms and hands. The big woman raised her hands in the air and fluttered them like bird wings, then folded them across her bosom. It was miserable being this close and not knowing what they were saying.

Suddenly Trixie slunk low to the ground with a warning growl. Trouble flattened out along beside her.

"Sh, sh," I said to them softly. "Pa said you weren't to make any fuss."

I quickly tied the rope holding the dogs to a sapling so I could watch the gypsy camp better.

Trixie growled again. Then I saw the end of a long stick pushing aside the clump of broom sage we were standing behind. The dogs leaped forward. Trixie grabbed the end of the long stick in her mouth, growling and baring her teeth. Liam, the gypsy boy, was hanging onto the other end. If I hadn't had the dogs tied to the sapling they would have had him before I could stop them.

"Let go!" I cried. "Let go and get back to the wagons before the dogs break loose!"

He let go the stick, but he stood there looking at me.

"Go!" I shouted.

"What do you mean, spying on our camp?"

"You're a liar. This is our land. I'm not spying on anybody," I yelled at him.

The dogs growled and strained against the rope.

"I'd take you on for spying on us if you didn't have those dogs."

"They're tied up. I'd like to see you, gypsy boy . . ."

The second I called him "gypsy boy" his eyes flashed and he came toward me.

He squatted, then dived for me, letting out a wild shriek. I jerked to one side before he hit me full force and he went down in a belly flop. Before I could turn he grabbed my foot and flipped me down with him. It knocked the breath out of me.

Trixie strained to the end of the rope and stood on her hind legs growling and snapping at Liam.

We rolled around in the broom sage, just out of reach of the dogs. At first Liam had the advantage. He got me face down with one arm twisted behind my back. He felt lighter than he looked and I tried bucking him up and off my back. We rolled over again and I came out on top. I managed to get astraddle of him and pinned his arms above his head.

"Give up, gypsy boy!" I cried in his face.

He twisted his head and spit at me.

I shook him hard.

He jerked his head up to spit again and I grabbed him by his hair. Liam let out a cry and started flinging his head from side to side. His long cap with the red tassel fell off and he suddenly stopped struggling and went limp.

What I saw turned me cold with fright. His head had a terrible gash in it. I pushed him away in horror, saying, "Oh my God, I've killed him."

When I looked more carefully I saw that his hair and the top of his head were cut away in the shape of a cross. I hadn't done that, but I must have hurt him when I grabbed him by the hair. The cut looked like it had been hacked out with a knife. It was festering and angry-looking.

"Liam, are you all right?" I called to the still body.

He sat up and reached for his cap. Then he

pulled it over that awful cut in his head. He was gritting his teeth hard and tears were sliding down his cheeks.

"Liam, what in the world . . ." I started to ask, but he scrambled up and ran toward the wagons.

"You're all alike!" he shouted over his shoulder as he ran.

I got the dogs quieted and sat down between them. They whimpered and nuzzled close. I put my arms around them and sat hidden in the broom sage wondering what in the world had happened to Liam's head.

In a few minutes Pa came back and said, "Let's go."

We started walking home and I kept waiting for Pa to tell me what he'd found out.

I couldn't stand it any longer, so I blurted out, "Pa, something's wrong down there. I just know it."

Pa took a deep breath and said, "We may be in for something I don't want to deal with."

We walked on, but Pa didn't offer to tell me any more. I kept sneaking glances at him and I thought he looked worried. He seemed to be far away, all wrapped up in his thoughts, like I wasn't walking along with him. I'd never seen Pa like that. It scared me.

I wished he would tell me what he'd found out,

but I was afraid to break in on him and ask outright. Finally, I said, "You know that gypsy boy I told you we met on the woods road? He's got a terrible gash cut in the top of his head—a gash shaped like a cross."

That pulled Pa out of it. He stopped and looked at me. "Harrison, don't tell anybody about this. Those folks there by the creek had a run-in with the Ku Klux Klan down in South Carolina. That's why they've turned back into North Carolina in the dead of winter."

NEW BROOMS

MY FEET WERE COLD. I SLID OUT OF BED and looked out of the window. Everything was covered with a silvery coat of frost. The sun was making the frost sparkle and dance so it almost blinded me. I squinched up my eyes and squinted at the washhouse roof shimmering in the frost-coated back yard.

Then I remembered—Little Hattie. "Come," she had said, "on the next big frost. Block on over if you want to go with me after broom sage."

I hadn't exactly promised to come for sure when

Little Hattie asked me, but that was before I knew what was going on down in the Hollow. I still couldn't put it all together. Pa had told Ma and Grandma last night that the gypsies wanted to camp by the creek until after Christmas. He said one of their women was ready to deliver a baby and they didn't want to make a long bumpy wagon trip till after the baby came. He didn't say a word to them about the Klan. I wondered if Pa was making up the business about the baby, since he hadn't mentioned that to me on the way home.

Right after breakfast I yelled to Aunt Het, "I'm going to Little Hattie's!" Then I took off before she could come up with a reason or an errand that would hold me back.

The bright morning sun cutting through the trees made lacy patterns on the tram road bed. My feet hardly touched the ground as I raced along. When I soared in a great leap over the rotting log that lay across the path, I was just a breath away from flying.

The sun shot through in a clear, solid shaft where the creek cut across the tram and the trestle ties sparkled with morning frost. "They're slick as ice," I thought to myself, "but I'm surefooted." I figured I could take the creek at a run.

I didn't slip on the trestle ties until I was one step from the bank, but that skid shot me safely onto solid ground. It knocked the breath out of me and the lightness out of my body, but only for a minute. I bounded along the rest of the way to Little Hattie's house feeling my usual self.

The door to her fireplace room was open, so I looked inside and called, "Little Hattie, you there?"

There was no answer and the room looked empty. I walked back to the porch and called again. A rattling noise sounded right under my feet. I almost jumped into the yard when I saw a yellow-flowered lump of cloth rising from under the porch. It swiveled toward me and a face smiled out of the front side of the flower-printed turban she had on her head. Little Hattie had a way of changing right before your eyes.

She laughed and stood up.

"How you like my traveling hat? Ain't it a block!"

"It's a block, all right. You nearly scared me half to death," I said hopping out in the yard to join her.

Little Hattie went through the business of lifting me off the ground.

She got me up, but she put me down with a grunt. "You blocking up some weight, Harrison child."

"What were you doing under the house?" I asked.

"Blocking out my tow sacks. Need them to bring back broom sage."

I was the only one around who didn't think Little Hattie was crazy. She seemed perfectly all right to me and for as long as I could remember she'd been my special friend. She was the only grown-up I knew who would give you straight answers. I guess you could say Little Hattie had been filling in the gaps in my education. All the things Ma and Grandma and Aunt Het whispered about, I could get straight from Little Hattie. She knew all the family secrets of the colored and the white and once you understood all her "blocking" talk she made a lot of sense.

I had a question for her. "What makes Mr. Bud Highsmith so mean? And why does he hate colored people?" I asked.

Little Hattie's eyes brightened and her face broke into a crooked smile—the kind she gets when there's a good story to tell.

"You don't know about Mat?" she asked.

"Know what about Mat?"

'Oh, child, that situation is a block. Mat and Bud Highsmith is natural sister and brother."

I was completely confused. "What Mat are you talking about?"

"I be talking about Mattie Davis. Miss Mattie Davis who runs the only colored boarding house in town. Mattie Davis who blocks the best pit-cooked barbecue, corn dodgers, and cole slaw you ever blocked a tooth into. That's Mr. Bud Highsmith's natural sister."

She stopped the story and picked up the tow sacks.

"You can't stop there. Tell me the rest of it." Little Hattie could drive you crazy with half a story.

"Ain't much more to tell. You asked me how come Bud Highsmith's such a mean block and don't like colored. Well, Mat's the answer."

"Come on, Little Hattie. You're holding out on me."

"I'll block it out for you straight. When Bud Highsmith's ma blocked on out of this life, his pa took up with Louvenia Davis, his colored cook. Well, he more than took up with her; they blocked out a baby girl. Bud was seven, maybe eight years old then. So he didn't think nothing of the light-skinned baby Louvenia brought with her in a R.C. Cola crate every day to the house. Fact is, Louvenia claimed Bud was fond of little Mattie.

"He must of been blocking on eleven years old before he found out Mat was his half-sister. Bud blocked real wild and tried to kill the little girl. And his pa nearly beat him to death. Louvenia told me if she died and blocked off to hell for her sins, she'd know what it was like. It would be like the day Bud tried to kill little Mattie and old man Highsmith tried to kill Bud. She said old man Highsmith beat Bud unmercifully and cursed his own child and tried to make him swear he'd never do harm to Mattie. But that Bud was a tough block and he wouldn't make no such promise. If Louvenia hadn't blocked into it and stood between them, old man Highsmith would more than likely have killed Bud."

She stopped the story and went into the kitchen.

"What happened?" I called after her.

"Need my cutting hook," she answered. "You gonna make me forget my cutting hook with all your questions."

Little Hattie came out with a short-handled, curved cutting hook.

"Didn't much happen after that. Louvenia moved off the Highsmith farm and old man Highsmith and Bud blocked out the next twenty years hating each other in the same house. Year before he died old man Highsmith bought Mattie a big house on the edge of town. That's how she come by her boarding house and barbecue place. Bud was so mad at his pa he wouldn't even bury him in a store-bought coffin. Had the colored folks make a homemade one and sent his pa blocking to glory, or wherever he went, in a pine board box.

"Now that Mat turned out to be a real block. She's got more money than any colored woman I know. People blocks in from miles around—colored and white—to buy her barbecue. She joshes all of them, tells a dirty joke or two, and I do believe she blocks out some bootleg liquor for them as wants it. And she ain't above letting anybody know she's half Highsmith. Yeah, I reckon Mat's the living cause of why Bud blocks so mean and hates colored so."

She headed out of the yard, and I knew that the Mat story was ended, as far as Little Hattie was concerned. I trotted after her turning the pieces of the story over in my head. I could follow Little Hattie's tale, blocks and all, but I still couldn t understand how you could hate somebody just because they were colored. I wished I could talk about it with Scrap and Kitty Fisher, but I couldn't find the words.

The story about Mat had me so caught up I'd forgotten to tell Little Hattie about the gypsies camped by the creek.

"We saw gypsies camped along the creek in Broomsage Hollow," I said.

"Yeah, I seen them blocking in here end of last summer."

"No, they're on the creek right now," I explained. "Kitty Fisher and Scrap and me saw them yesterday."

Little Hattie stopped. "Night before last I had that dream. That fiery dream. That's when they blocked in here. I had a sign, a warning sign. I bet you a block that's when they moved in."

"Well, you'll see them when we get to Broomsage Hollow," I said.

When we reached the Hollow the wagons were there, strung out along the creek bank, but not a soul was in sight.

We stayed on the far side of the Hollow where the broom sage grew the tallest. I held big bunches of it and Little Hattie whacked them off near the ground with her cutting hook.

"Frost that blocked in here last night set the broom sage good," said Little Hattie. "Now it won't shed all over the floor when you start to sweep."

Soon we had two large tow sacks filled with first rate broom sage. Little Hattie stopped cutting and stood staring at the wagons.

"Think we ought to block down there and see if they's anybody around?" she asked.

A PREDICTION

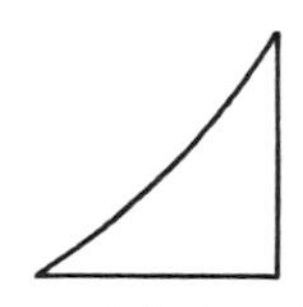

I WAS EXCITED, EVEN A LITTLE NERVOUS, as we plowed through the broom sage toward the wagons.

Little Hattie marched up to the large wagon and called out, "Anybody home? Anybody blocking in there?"

The door of the shack cracked open a slit. It was dark inside and we couldn't see who was there. After a few moments the door opened wider. The sunlight swept in and the huge woman Pa had talked with hobbled into the open doorway. A young woman with long yellow hair appeared behind the old woman and placed a fringed shawl around her shoulders. Now that I was up close I saw that the big woman was old—very old. She was creased and wrinkled and brown, but sharp blue eyes like Liam's sparkled under her sagging eyelids.

"Morning," said Little Hattie.

"Morning," I repeated.

The old woman and the young woman nodded their heads. "Blessings of the holy season," said the old woman.

Little Hattie pulled a good handful of broom sage from one of the tow sacks. She reached into her pocket and brought out a long red string. With lightning speed she wound the red string around the bunch of broom sage and knotted it with a flourish at the top of the broom. Then she handed it to the old woman.

"Christmas gift to you," she said.

The gypsy woman took the broom and replied, "A new broom is a sign of friendship. I thank you."

"What you be doing blocking through here this time of year?" asked Little Hattie.

"We are following a dark and dangerous fate," replied the old woman.

"We ran into some trouble in South Carolina," explained the young woman.

I wondered if she meant the Klan. I hadn't told Little Hattie about that.

The old woman sat down in the doorway with a grunt.

"My bones are too old for this chilly weather," she said, pulling the shawl tighter around her shoulders. "I need strong sun for the days remaining to me."

After the old woman sat down I could see what a big belly the young woman had. I figured she must be the one that was soon to have a baby.

"It's all my fault, Grandmother," said the young woman. "Soon we'll move toward the sun again. Soon."

The old woman squinted her eyes and stared hard at me. "Child," she said, "you're a part of it. Yes, I can see it. Stamped right there on your forehead. You're a part of it."

I rubbed my forehead to see if it was dirty or something. I didn't like the way the old woman stared at me.

"What am I a part of?" I blurted out.

"A dark fate that dogs us, even in this holy season. I don't get it clear, but you're there, and you're part of it."

"You some kind of fortune-teller?" asked Little Hattie.

"I'm blessed with some powers of divination," answered the old woman. "I hold that power in this traveling group."

What did she mean by "power of divination"? If she had power she must be some kind of leader.

"Are you the queen of this group?" I asked.

The old woman laughed.

"Everybody's got a name for it. Nay, child, I'm no queen—just the vessel that carries the power of foresight for a time." She sighed heavily. "I've carried it long and I've waited patiently for the sign to pass it on. But the sign is not yet revealed."

Then she squinted at me again. "Can't get that sign clear. Not the way I see the one on your forehead. That one's sharp and clear. And soon to follow."

I was beginning to feel cold and uneasy, even though the sun was shining.

"What sign you be blocking after?" asked Little Hattie.

The old woman answered as if she understood perfectly well Little Hattie's peculiar way of talking. "I'm waiting for a child," she said; "a child born under the sign of the veil, to pass on my gift. No way to rest these bones till that child comes. Dear Jesus, send it soon."

She closed her sagging eyelids and rocked gently back and forth.

"Where's everybody?" I asked.

The young woman with the long yellow hair said, "Men are all gone off looking for tinkering jobs."

The old woman started to hum as she rocked, eyes still closed. I pulled at Little Hattie's arm and motioned her to let's go.

As we were leaving, the young woman called out, "My name's Mrs. Kathleen Cafferty. I didn't get yours."

Little Hattie kept moving into the broom sage, but I shouted over my shoulder, "I'm Harrison Hawkins and this is my friend Little Hattie George."

At Little Hattie's house we sat on the porch and wound red and green strips of cloth around the bunches of broom sage. The pile of golden straw brooms with their colorful wrappings looked real Christmasy. On Christmas morning Little Hattie would visit every farmhouse in the neighborhood with her brooms.

"Christmas gift!" she'd cry handing out her brooms.

And as her tow sack lost brooms it would fill up with oranges, apples, raisins, nuts, and sometimes a little pocket change. Ma took three or four brooms, so she always gave some change along with the Christmas treats.

I was thinking about the gypsies. Kathleen Cafferty had the same last name as Liam. I wondered if they were kin. They sure didn't look alike. And the old woman who had the power of foresight was still puzzling me.

"Why do you reckon those folks camped in the hollow don't like to be called gypsies?" I asked.

"Didn't know they objected," answered Little Hattie.

"Well, the gypsy boy I met acted real mad when I called his family gypsies."

"It be my guess that they don't block being called gypsies any more than us colored folks likes being called niggers."

"He said they were tinkers—Irish tinkers."

"Maybe tinkers is what they would like you to call them. Or just their Christian names would do."

Little Hattie looked at me sideways.

"They's still something about them gypsies you ain't blocked out to me," she said. "What you holding back, Harrison child?"

"They told Pa they had a run-in with the Ku Klux Klan over in South Carolina and had to turn back into North Carolina."

"Ain't that a block!" cried Little Hattie, slapping her thigh. "Does Bud Highsmith know they's down by the creek?"

"They're on Pa's land. I don't think so, why?"

"That Bud's a Klanner. Mat told me so."

"But there's no Klan in North Carolina. It's outlawed here."

"Child, we be blocking right on the South Carolina border and they's plenty that follows the Klan around here. Secret Klanners be all around here. They guards it careful."

I looked at Little Hattie, wondering whether to believe what I was hearing.

She leaned close to me and whispered in my ear,

"Could be one in your own family and you'd never know it."

I didn't like what she was saying. I pulled away. "What are you whispering for? There's nobody around."

Little Hattie laughed; then she suddenly stopped. She frowned and her eyes moved from me to some far-off place. "That Bud's one of them, all right. I hope he don't find out them pore souls is blocking down by the creek."

Little Hattie looked scared. Why was everybody so scared when the Klan was mentioned? I had a yearning to talk to Pa. When I stood up I could see my shadow was straight under my feet.

"Look!" I cried. "It's twelve o'clock already. I got to get home for dinner."

"Block careful, child," Little Hattie called after me as I ran from her yard.

Pa was in the big barn when I found him. Pa and one of the gypsy tinkers and Liam. They were working on one of old Maud's shoes. Maud's an old mule of ours and her hooves crack and she keeps losing shoes.

"Aye, you can bet that'll be holding her for a while," said the gypsy man.

Pa dug into his pocket and handed the man a dollar bill.

"My thanks," said the man. "If you should be needing knives or scissors sharpened or any kind of metal mended I can do the job."

Pa said, "Thank you, Mr. Cafferty. There's some harness that needs repairing. Let's take a look at it and see if you can handle it."

Liam started packing up their tools in an old bag that looked like it was made out of a piece of fancy rug. None of them had seen me standing behind the front gate to the barn. I don't know why I didn't let them know I was there. Something held me back. Pa was still talking with Mr. Cafferty and I was watching Liam. I saw him when he slid Pa's short crowbar into the bag. He closed it up and started toward the gate where I was standing. I moved back to the side of the barn where he couldn't see me.

The minute he was outside the gate with the bag, I stepped up behind him and said, "All right. Liam, give me Pa's crowbar."

He looked at me with those sharp blue eyes just the way a caught rabbit would when I reached in to take it out of the trap.

"I saw you put it in that bag," I said.

I wondered if we were going to have another fight right there in front of Pa and the tinker man.

First he acted like he was going to make a run for it. Then he looked back toward the barn and reached into the carpet bag and snatched out the crowbar. He slammed it on the ground in a real mean way.

"We need such a crowbar for prying wheels off

the wagons," he said.

I picked up the crowbar and mumbled something about stealing under my breath.

"Ain't no sin for us to take things we need," he said.

"And what gives you any special rights?" I asked him.

He still looked like he was going to bolt out of the barnyard. And I was sure he would have given me another fight if we had been alone on the woods road.

"We had the right since Christ died," he answered me.

"What are you talking about?"

"It was tinkers like us that was asked to make the spikes to nail Christ on the cross," he explained.

"I don't see how that gives you any right to take Pa's crowbar."

"They asked the tinkers to make four spikes. And four they made. But on the way to Calvary where they nailed Christ to the cross, the tinkers stole back one of the nails. And our Lord was spared the pain of that spike. Ever since, we been given the right to take what we need."

I couldn't believe my ears. And I wondered if Liam was just a good liar in a tight spot, or if there was something to what he was telling me.

Just then Pa and the tinker man came out of the barn.

"This is Mr. Tom Cafferty," Pa said to me. "And I see you've already met his brother Liam."

The Cafferty brothers took off and I picked up Pa's crowbar. But I didn't mention anything to Pa about it.

On the way to the house I said to Pa, "Did you know Mr. Bud Highsmith's a Klanner?"

Pa looked at me with a frown on his face. "Who told you that?"

"Little Hattie said it was so. She got it straight from Mattie Davis, Mr. Bud's half-sister."

Pa stopped in his tracks. "It appears Little Hattie's been bringing you up to date on a lot of things."

I knew I'd let too much out the minute I'd said it.

Pa said, "Now you listen to me, Harrison. I don't want you repeating any of this business about Mr. Highsmith or the Klan. Do you hear me? Stay away from that gypsy camp—I strictly forbid you to go there. And forget you ever heard the name of Ku Klux Klan."

We walked on to the house in silence. The sweet, spicy smell of fruitcakes baking floated out and played around my nose. But I was worried and wondering. Wondering why Pa was so sharp with me. It wasn't like Pa—and I didn't dare mention to him that I'd already been back to the gypsy camp—and that the old woman had said I was a part of their fate.

CEDAR TREE

A THE FRUITCAKES WERE LAID OUT ON THE long table on the back porch. They had cooled overnight and Grandma had set me to poking holes in them with a toothpick.

"Punch the toothpick all the way in," called Grandma from the kitchen.

She came out on the porch carrying a quart jar of rosy homemade grape wine and a bottle of Welch's Grape Juice.

"Now, I want to give them a good soaking before they're wrapped," she said as she dribbled wine over the ones I'd poked full of holes.

She handed me the bottle of Welch's Grape Juice. "Here, Harrison, soak yours with this." I guess Grandma didn't trust me with a wine-soaked cake all my own.

Ma joined us and admired the cakes. "It's only five days until Christmas," she reminded us, "and we don't have a tree yet."

"Kitty Fisher, Scrap, and me are going today to find Christmas trees," I answered. "We'll pick a good one."

"Look for some princess pine too," said Ma. "I want to make a wreath for the front door. And see if you can find some mistletoe."

"Which woods we gonna search in?" asked Kitty Fisher.

"Depends on the tree," I replied.

"Ma said for me and Kitty to pick a holly. If we fin' one with lots of red berries, it will be already decorated," said Scrap.

"I was thinking of something else for our tree," I said.

"Well, what did you have in mind?" asked Kitty.

"What about a nice cedar tree?" I asked.

"Cedars is bad luck," said Scrap.

"Bad luck? How can a tree be bad luck?" I asked.

"They say if you plant a cedar tree you'll die when it makes a shadow big enough to cover your grave," Scrap explained.

"They say. Who's *they say?*" I asked. "That's dumb. Silliest thing I know of."

I laughed at Scrap, but she looked very serious and said, "How come the only cedar trees I see planted around here be growing in the graveyard? Besides, it's bad luck to cut one down, same as planting one."

"Well, maybe you don't want to come with us, because I've got my head set on a cedar tree," I answered

She looked doubtful for a moment. Then she broke into a grin and said, "I don't believe in bad luck that much."

"Which way we going?" asked Kitty Fisher.

"I saw lots of holly trees and some pretty cedars growing along the woods road the other day," I said.

"Yeah, me too," said Kitty, "but all the cedars was on old man Highsmith's side."

"We can stay in the woods on Pa's side. There's got to be at least one good cedar there," I argued.

I didn't tell Kitty Fisher and Scrap the real reason I was determined to have a cedar tree for Christmas. The woods road led to Broomsage Hollow and the gypsy camp. Pa had forbidden me to go to the camp, but you could sure check it out looking for a Christmas tree.

Kitty was right. We kept finding nice-shaped cedars on Mr. Highsmith's side of the road. But none on Pa's side.

There were plenty of hollies on our side, but Scrap kept turning them down. "Not enough berries . . . too tall and skinny . . . lopsided . . . not just right."

"That beats all I've ever seen," I complained. "These cedars must think it's bad luck to grow on our side of the road.'

"Well, princess pine don't," shouted Scrap "Here's a good patch."

We gathered more than enough of the dark green vines to make Ma's wreath. In the same patch there was a big oak tree with lots of pale green mistletoe with clusters of little white berries growing on its bare branches.

"Give me a boost," I said to Kitty Fisher. "There's some pretty mistletoe up there."

Kitty looked up. "No sireee!" he cried. "I ain't giving you no boost up a tree. Your luck in trees is bad these days. I'll get that mistletoe myself."

Kitty got the mistletoe out of the oak tree and we went on down the woods road looking for a cedar and a holly to please Scrap. Around the next bend we found the "just right" holly. It was loaded with bright red berries. Scrap pointed to it, smiled, and nodded her head. Kitty chopped it down. We trimmed the branches, and I helped Kitty carry the tree carefully to keep from knocking the berries off.

Cedars kept popping up on Mr. Highsmith's

property like they were daring us to come over and take one.

We were almost at the end of the woods road before we found it. A wonderful dark green cedar, about eight feet tall, beautifully shaped and looking like all the Christmas card trees you've ever seen. And it was growing on Pa's side of the road.

"There it is!" I shouted.

Scrap and Kitty Fisher had to agree. This was it; better than any on Mr. Bud's side of the road. This was the perfect Christmas tree. We cut away some of the bottom limbs and chopped it down. The tree had a wonderful smell, clean and fresh and spicy.

"I'll drag the cedar," I said. "Scrap, you help Kitty carry the holly."

Back on the woods road I turned toward Broomsage Hollow.

"We going home that way?" asked Kitty Fisher.

"Yeah," I replied. "We're almost to the Hollow now; might as well go on that way."

"We ain't messing around with them gypsies," said Scrap.

"Who said anything about gypsies," I asked, trying to sound surprised she had brought it up.

"Ma said for us to stay away from that camp," she added.

"Well, Pa told me the same thing. We're not going to the camp. Can I help it if you can see the camp across the Hollow? That's not going to the camp."

"Well, not exactly," said Kitty Fisher.

We made the last turn in the road before Broomsage Hollow and Kitty, who was carrying the front end of the holly tree, stopped suddenly. It made Scrap stumble because he didn't warn her he was stopping.

"Can't you give a warning . . ."

Kitty dropped his end of the tree.

"Sh-sh," he whispered with a finger to his lips.

He pointed to a pickup truck and a Model A Ford parked at the edge of Broomsage Hollow.

"That's old man Highsmith's truck," he whispered.

"Haul ass out of here the other way," hissed Scrap. "That mean old man ain't never gonna believe we didn't take one of his cedars. I told you they was bad luck trees."

"Hush!" I said. "Get off the road. Let's sneak through the woods and see what he's doing in the Hollow. That Hollow's Pa's land. I know he's up to something."

Scrap and Kitty Fisher looked like they didn't want to find out.

"Come on," I urged. "He'll never know we're here. Besides, we can outrun him in the woods anyway."

They still didn't look too eager, but Kitty picked up one end of the tree, I took the other, and we moved off the road into the thick woods. Scrap followed us.

"Let's leave the trees here," I said. "We can sneak in closer and quieter without them."

Scrap looked at me and groaned. "Harrison, you asking for a bunch of trouble. I don't know why we's following you." Then she smiled and said, "But we is."

Kitty Fisher nodded his head and stuck his thumb into his mouth. He always does that when he's worried about something or thinking hard. Me and Scrap usually tease him about it, but this time I didn't say anything.

We crept through the soft pine straw that covered the ground until we were close to the cars.

Mr. Bud Highsmith was standing in front of his truck with a strange man. He was pointing toward the gypsy camp and talking to the stranger. I could make out the license plate on the Model A Ford. It was a different color from our plates and said South Carolina, '36.

We were hidden behind some thick myrtle bushes that grew close to the ground, but we were still too far to make out what they were saying.

"I'm scooting closer so I can hear," I whispered to Scrap and Kitty. Then I slithered on my belly to where there was just one row of thick myrtles between me and them. Kitty and Scrap slid into place on either side of me. This was no time to say "Eskimo Pie," but I thought of it.

Mr. Bud was talking.

". . . didn't want to mention any of this on the telephone when I called you," said Mr. Bud. "That central operator listens in to any long distance calls, so I had to play it real tight."

"We're used to reading between the lines, Brother Highsmith," said the strange man. "I knew it was important or you wouldn't be telephoning."

I wondered why the man was calling Mr. Highsmith, *Brother*. Little Hattie told me Mr. Bud didn't have any brothers or sisters, other than his half-sister, Mattie Davis.

"We'll be more than pleased to remove this nuisance from around here," said the stranger. "We got some unfinished business to settle with this bunch anyhow. The brothers didn't get that gypsy they were after down in South Carolina. It's no good letting them think they can get away with a thing like that. We've got to let them know that the long arm of the Klan reaches out wherever they run."

"A little show would kill two birds at one shot," said Mr. Bud. "The niggers need a good scaring too. Without it they get out of line. It's been a good while since they had a reminder, and a lot of them ain't keeping to their proper place. Yes sir, Brother Jake, come to think of it, cleaning out that nest of thieving Catholic gypsies would have a healthy effect on uppity niggers and some nigger-loving whites I know around here."

"You're right, Brother Bud. Some folks forgits what the three K's stand for–Koons, Kathlics, and Kikes. Long as we keep the niggers, the Pope worshippers and the Jews in line, this'll be a decent place to bring up children."

Kitty Fisher tugged at my shirt. "Let's get out of here," he whispered.

"Don't stir," I whispered back. "They might hear us. Keep down and keep quiet. We've got to wait it out now."

"How about if we make it a present on Christmas night?" said the man Mr. Bud called Brother Jake.

"Can't think of a nicer gift on the birthday of our Christ," said Mr. Bud. "You've got the lay of the land. I'll have my boys ready to join you. We have to keep it undercover here, you understand. But we'll be backing you up all the way. This is God's country, and it's our duty to keep it a decent place to bring up children."

Brother Jake and Mr. Bud did some kind of strange handshake. Then they climbed into their cars and drove off.

We stayed still until they were out of sight. I felt stiff from not moving for so long.

"What did that man mean by kikes?" asked Scrap. "Did he mean them gypsies down there?"

"No," I answered. "I reckon he's after the gypsies because they're Catholics. I believe he said kikes were Jews."

"Well, you heard who he put on the top of the list," said Kitty Fisher. "Them koons they was talking about is us."

I didn't know what to answer Kitty. I was embarrassed to even say the word "koons."

"Let's go back the way we came," I said. "I'm going to tell Pa what we heard. And I don't want to say we went by the gypsy camp."

We were quiet carrying the trees and the Christmas greens back to the house. I don't know why, but the ugly things those men said had put a distance between me and my friends. I felt guilty the same way as I did in school when the teacher said. "All right, we're going to sit without any talking until the guilty one raises his hand." Even when I didn't know a thing about it, I felt guilty. On the silent trip home, I felt that way—only worse.

Kitty Fisher and Scrap took off with the holly tree as soon as we got back. I think they were eager to get home and tell their folks what they'd heard.

Ma and Grandma "oh'ed" and "ah'ed" over the beautiful cedar while we were setting it up in the living room. But I couldn't get too excited about it. My mind was on Mr. Bud and Brother Jake, and I needed to talk to Pa about it.

Pa finally came back from town about the middle of the afternoon, and I spent another miserable hour before I could catch him alone. At last I got my chance when he went to the smokehouse to get a cured ham for Aunt Het.

"Pa, there's something awful about to happen to those gypsies."

"I thought I told you to stay away from there," said Pa sharply.

"I didn't go to the camp. But we heard Mr. Bud Highsmith and a man called Brother Jake talking about cleaning out a nest of thieving gypsies."

"Where did you hear such a thing?"

"On the woods road, when we were looking for the Christmas tree."

"Does Bud Highsmith know you heard him?"

Pa had such a worried look on his face it bothered me.

"No, Pa, I'm sure. He never saw us at all."

"So Scrap and Kitty Fisher heard it too?"

"Yes, Pa, they did. What does it mean, Pa?"

"Have you mentioned this to your Ma and Grandma?"

"No, Pa."

"First, Harrison, you tell me every word you heard. Think hard now and tell me everything you can remember."

I told Pa the whole thing including the part about koons, kathlics and kikes.

"What are we going to do?" I asked Pa when I was finished.

Pa looked strange. I'd never seen him with a look like that on his face. I realized he was scared. My Pa, scared. What was the matter? I'd never seen Pa scared in my whole life. It made mc feel uneasy, like someone had stolen something from me I'd always depended on. I couldn't look at him.

Pa still hadn't answered my question. I was staring at the ground, but I asked him again.

"What are we going to do, Pa?"

"Keep out of this, Harrison. I'm sorry you've gotten mixed up with this mess. I don't want you to say a word about any of this to anybody, not even to Ma or Grandma. And we won't speak another word about it. You could cause a lot of people to get hurt."

What was Pa accusing me of? How could I cause anyone to get hurt? I needed to ask him so many questions. But Pa was suddenly different. I knew I couldn't talk to him now.

"I've got to run back to town," said Pa.

He'd just come from town. I didn't understand.

"That tinker man, Tom Cafferty, is apt to bring back the harnesses while I'm gone."

Pa pulled a couple of dollar bills from his pocket and handed them to me. "Check the harness for me and see that he's done a good job. Then give him this money. But not a word about the Highsmith business."

My stomach felt funny. Was Pa just going to let it happen? My pa who took such good care of strangers? My pa who'd never been scared of anything?

"All right, Pa," I said. But I still couldn't look at him.

TAROT CARDS

I HUNG AROUND THE BARN THE REST OF the afternoon waiting for Tom Cafferty. It was getting late and I thought maybe he wasn't coming. Just as I was about ready to give up and head for the house, Liam turned into the lane. He was by himself and he was carrying the harnesses.

When he saw me he pulled up short and stood there in the lane gate with his sharp eyes checking everything out.

"Come on in," I called to him, ' I'm not going to sic the dogs on you."

"I brought Mr. Hawkins the harness," he said, still not budging.

"Pa's not home, but you can leave it with me."

Finally he moved inside the gate.

"My brother fixed it," he said, handing over the heavy bundle of leather reins with brass fittings.

I spread it out on the ground so I could check it. Liam stood a little to one side, still eyeing me as if he thought I might jump him any minute.

"Looks good as new," I told him.

"Tom's a fine tinker," he said.

I dug into my pocket and brought out the two bills.

"Pa said to give you this."

"My thanks," he said. But he didn't turn and go. He acted like he wanted to hang around and talk.

"How long your folks planning on staying down by the creek?" I asked.

"'Til the baby comes," answered Liam.

"Whose baby?"

"Tom and his wife, Kathleen. I'll be an uncle then."

"When's the baby due?"

"Right now," said Liam.

I couldn't think of any more questions. We were silent for a few moments and I thought he was getting ready to leave. Suddenly I noticed a pack of cards jammed into his jacket pocket.

"What kind of cards are those?"

"Tarot cards," he replied.

"Tarot? What kind is that?"

Liam pulled the thick pack from his pocket. They were bigger than a regular playing deck. He shuffled the cards, making them flash through his hands with a clicking sound. I'd tried that with cards but they always flew all over the place.

"These cards tell your whole future," he said.

"Are they fortune-telling cards?"

"They tell the future, if you know how to read them," he answered.

"Can you read them?"

Liam looked hard at me and almost smiled. "A little," he said.

"Show me how you do it."

He handed me the cards.

"Shuffle them," he said.

I fumbled through them as best as I could.

"Now draw three cards out of the deck," he said.

I pulled three cards and started to look at them.

"No!" he shouted. "Don't look. Turn them upside down and put them back in the deck."

After I stuck them back in he said, "Now shuffle them again and lay the cards down."

We both squatted on the ground and I laid the cards between us.

"What's your birth date?" he asked.

"November fifteen, nineteen twenty-five," I told him.

"I'm a year older than you," he said.

Then he picked up a small stick and wrote a bunch of numbers on the ground.

"I'm using the month, the day, and the year to get your number," he explained.

In a few seconds he said, "Seven. That's your number. Seven is the chariot card."

He handed me the deck and said, "Go through and find the picture of the man in a chariot."

I started flipping through the cards. What I thought was the chariot turned up on the third card. I held it up to ask Liam if it was the right one, but a sudden quirky little whirlwind blew it out of my hand.

Liam scrambled to recover the card.

"Was it upside down?" he asked.

"I don't know. I didn't check."

"It's very important to know if the card was upside down," he said, sounding irritated with me. "I'll have to give you both readings if you don't know."

"What do you mean?"

"Everything the card stands for is reversed if the card's upside down," explained Liam.

"Can't we do it over?"

"No," he snapped sharply.

Then his keen blue eyes seemed to bore into the chariot card. After a moment he turned it so I could see the picture. "It means you will shield someone from harm. It means you will bring safety," he said.

He pointed to a section of the card. "Here are trees and a stream of water. Maybe you will bring safety to a place like that."

Then his fingers slid toward the top of the card. "There is an azure curtain of silver stars over the chariot. It means you will help someone at night."

Finally he pointed to the bottom of the card where a pair of sphinxes were hitched to the chariot. "The sphinx stands for a riddle. You have a riddle that puzzles you. And you don't know how to solve it. Soon you will learn the answer."

I was about to ask him a question, but he held up his hand and said, "That's what your card means *unless* it was in the deck upside down. If it was upside down you will betray someone. You will fail to bring help when someone is in need. Misfortune will follow wherever you go."

Liam pushed the chariot card back into the deck and deftly shuffled the cards. Then he returned them to his pocket.

"What does it—"

I didn't finish my question before he said, "That's all I can tell you. That's as far as I can go in the cards."

Another little December whirlwind flicked by us, trailing a few dry pecan leaves. We stood up.

"Would you like some pecans?" I asked. "We

could pick up a bucketful in no time right here in the yard."

Liam hesitated for a moment and I could tell he was about to say no.

"In payment for your card reading I'll take some pecans," he said.

I grabbed a bucket and we started gathering pecans.

"Are you Catholic?" I asked.

"Aye," he said, "that we are."

"My family's Missionary Baptist," I told him.

He stopped picking up pecans and looked at me. "Kathleen's family is Missionary Baptist. They've caused us a lot of trouble."

"Well, it doesn't matter to me what people are," I told him, "It seems like a lot of fuss over nothing to me. Do you like Kathleen?"

"Aye, I do. She's good to me. And she cooks a lot better than Tom."

"Why was your brother cooking?"

"Our Ma is dead."

We had the bucket filled with pecans.

Liam stared off into space and spoke as if he was talking to himself. "That baby's caused a lot of trouble."

"You said it wasn't even born. How can it cause trouble?"

"My brother's wife is not one of us."

"I don't get you."

"She's not from a tinker family. She run off with my brother and married him against her family."

"Where does your brother's wife come from?"

"From near Beaufort, South Carolina. We used to camp near there every year for a week or so. Tom met her a couple of years ago, and they got married last year when we were there. Her folks was fit to kill."

"But you said the baby caused trouble?"

"Aye, it was the baby."

I remembered Kathleen. She was the woman with the long yellow hair I had met in the tinkers' camp.

Liam was still talking. "She wanted to have the baby near home. She said if her mother saw the baby, they could make it up. So we went back to our old camp near Beaufort."

"What happened?"

Liam pulled off his cap and bent his head forward, showing me the ugly festering cut. "This is what happened. The Ku Klux Klan paid us a visit. A warning visit, they said. They came when all of the men were out of the camp. And they burned a cross in front of our wagon. They said Tom would never get away with stealing Kathleen from her folks. I tried to tear the cross down and they grabbed me and did this to my head."

He put his cap back on.

"We been moving north for a week to get out of South Carolina. My brother told Kathleen that it's better to bear with a mite of cold and have our Christmas in peace while we wait for the baby. He savs we're safe now."

I wanted to shout, "No, Liam, no! You're not safe!" But I couldn't. I couldn't go back on Pa's orders. I'd never done that. I didn't know what to say, but I had to say something.

"Maybe you can come by again before your folks leave the Hollow," I said. "Maybe you could show me some more in the cards?"

"Aye, maybe," he replied.

"Maybe you could tell me about all the places you've been. Things you've seen and done."

"Aye, maybe," he replied, "but I don't trust outsiders."

"You can trust me. We've had our fight. Now we can be friends."

"Listen, Missionary Baptist boy," said Liam in a harsh voice, "I wouldn't trust you as far as I can throw this bucket of pecans. I've traveled up and down and far and wide and the one thing I've learned is: stick to your own; don't trust outsiders; you'll end up sorry."

I was beginning to get mad at him. But I did want to be his friend. I wanted him to be friends with me and Kitty Fisher and Scrap. I didn't know how to answer him.

"Well, I reckon I won't be seeing you again," I said.

Liam looked at the sinking sun. "Night comes

on fast," he said. "I'd better get going. Thanks for the pecans. Maybe you will see me again. I'll come back to return the bucket."

Then he smiled. The first time I'd seen him smile. "I don't steal everything," he said. "We don't have a good crowbar, but we got plenty of buckets."

As I walked back to the house I remembered Pa's strict orders about not going to the gypsy camp, about not talking about the Klan. And the scared look on his face came back to haunt me. The sun was suddenly gone, and it felt cold. I shivered and ran toward the warm, safe light coming from our kitchen window.

KKK

GRANDMA AND MA AND AUNT HET WENT into high gear on Friday.

"Only two days left 'til Christmas." Grandma sighed. "Will we ever get it all done?"

"If we stopped right now, we'd have enough to hold a army through Christmas," said Aunt Het.

"But we haven't made any lizzies or lady fingers. And, oh my lord, I forgot about the fresh coconut pies. Where's Harrison?" she called from the kitchen door.

"Right here, Grandma," I answered.

Me and Scrap and Kitty Fisher were in the back yard dipping sweet gum balls in gold paint for Ma's door wreath.

"Harrison," Grandma shouted, "come in here and get these coconuts. They've got to be cracked and worried out of their shells."

She handed me a large dishpan with three big brown coconuts, an ice pick, and a couple of paring knives.

"Drive a hole in with the pick and drain out the milk before you crack them," she said. "Here's a jar for the milk."

While Scrap finished dipping the sweet gum balls, me and Kitty Fisher tackled the coconuts. We cracked them with the ax and started prying out the sweet milky coconut meat.

"These things be worse than black walnuts," said Kitty Fisher, digging into the cracked pieces of coconut.

I wanted to tell Kitty Fisher about Liam and the tarot cards. Maybe Kitty would have an idea about how to make friends with the gypsy boy. But I was afraid to mention it, even to Kitty. I had this crazy notion in my head that if I didn't tell a soul, a way would turn up for me to work it out myself.

So I asked Kitty instead, "What's Santa Claus bringing you this year?"

"Shoot, you know there ain't no Santy Claus," said Kitty Fisher.

"I know there's no Santa Claus, but I keep quiet about it not to disappoint Ma and Grandma."

"My ma says we's too old and too poor to pretend there be one."

"Well, you're going to get something, aren't you?" I asked.

Scrap bounced over just as I asked the question.

"Yeah, we's getting something, all right," she butted in. "New underwear."

"Who'd ever ask Santy Claus for new underwear?" added Kitty.

"Well, it ain't exactly the kind of Christmas present you go around showing your friends at school," said Scrap.

"What you getting?" asked Kitty.

Suddenly I was sorry I had brought up the whole thing. I was ashamed to say what I was getting. But I had to tell them now.

"I'm getting an electric wood-burning set."

"What's that?" asked Kitty Fisher.

"It's a thing like a big pencil that you plug in and you can burn pictures into wood with it. Or, you can make signs."

Kitty and Scrap didn't say anything.

"I'll let you try it out after Christmas," I told them.

They still didn't say anything.

Grandma called from the house to ask about the coconut.

"Yes," I answered, "we got it out of the shell I'm bringing it in."

The telephone was ringing when I reached the kitchen. Two shorts and a long. That was our number on the party line. The ringing repeated—short-short-long.

"Harrison, would you answer that telephone," called Grandma. "Hateful thing would ring just as I get my hands into lady-finger dough."

I ran into the hall and shouted, "Hello!" into the phone.

The central operator said she had a long-distance call for Pa from Latta, South Carolina. My heart started to thump.

"He's gone to town and won't be back until late this afternoon," I told the central.

She said to tell him to call the central operator in Latta, South Carolina, when he got back.

My heart beats fast when we get a long-distance call. To me long-distance calls always mean something bad. When I was little they called from Florida to tell Ma that her sister Sadie was dead. Ma fainted right at the phone. I'll never forget seeing the receiver dangle loose from the wall and Ma lying on the floor under it.

I told Grandma what the central operator said.

"Peculiar," was all she said, and went on rolling out lady-finger dough. I went back in the yard where Kitty and Scrap were dipping the last of the sweet gum balls.

Pa had ordered me not to talk about the Klan, but he couldn't have meant that to include Kitty and Scrap. They already knew about it.

"Did you tell your folks what we heard at Broomsage Hollow?" I asked them.

"Yeah," said Kitty Fisher, "we told them."

"Well, what did they say?"

"They said not to talk about it," answered Kitty.

"Papa went to all the colored families around here and told them to watch out over Christmas," said Scrap. "He got out the shotgun to show Mama how—"

"Hush up," warned Kitty, "we ain't supposed to talk about it."

I couldn't understand why Kitty was hushing Scrap. It was all right not to tell the grown-ups, or some other kids, but we'd always told each other everything. I was put out by it. Then I remembered that I wasn't telling them about Liam's visit.

I blurted out the main thing that was bothering me. "You think anybody's going to warn the gypsies?"

"We got strict orders not to go near there," said Kitty Fisher.

"Seems like everybody's got strict orders," I said angrily. "Seems like everybody's scared to death. The least I expected was I could count on you."

"What you hollering about?" asked Kitty Fisher. "What you mean you can't count on us?"

"Well, it looks like your pa and my pa and everybody else around here is so scared of the Klan they won't dare go down there and warn those gypsies of what's coming. And since they won't do it I was counting on us."

Kitty Fisher and Scrap looked at me like I'd gone crazy.

"Harrison, is you colorblind?" asked Scrap.

"No. What do you mean colorblind?"

"Well, what color you think me and Kitty is?"

"You're my best friends," I answered.

"That ain't what I asked you."

I couldn't answer. I couldn't bring myself to say the word "black."

"We's them koons they was talking about," said Kitty Fisher. "And Papa says they's just itching for us to make one little wrong move. You got a lot of concern for them gypsies. What about *us?* I don't want my papa strung up by no night riders 'cause I warned some gypsies I don't even know."

"Well, I reckon there's nobody I can count on, then."

Scrap and Kitty Fisher were quiet for a few moments. Kitty's finger popped into his mouth, and Scrap kept stubbing the ground with the toe of her shoe.

"We didn't say you couldn't count on us," Scrap

said very quietly. "Kitty just told you what a bind we's in."

"Yeah, I reckon everybody's in a bind," I said.

Pa rang up the central operator as soon as he got home. There was something about that long distance call that made me stick around to hear what Pa would say. In my mind I kept hearing Liam say, "The sphinx means you have a riddle. Soon you will learn the answer."

I picked up a copy of *The Progressive Farmer* and plunked down on the couch near the door that opened into the hall. Pa was still talking with the central operator when I sat down on the couch. I pretended I was reading the magazine.

Finally Pa had the party who had been trying to call him on the phone.

"No names like we agreed," said Pa.

The person at the other end must have said something because Pa was quiet for a while.

"Yes, they're still here. When will you be ready?"

There was a pause.

"About a dozen," said Pa. "We need to take care of a dozen families."

During the next silence I was trying to figure out what the other party was saying.

"You're right, we've got to keep this a decent place to bring up children," said Pa.

My heart started to beat fast. That was the same

thing Brother Jake had said to Mr. Bud Highsmith! A terrible thought flushed hot over me. I couldn't believe such a thing. But it had crept into my mind. Could Pa? Little Hattie's words, "Could be one in your own family and you'd never know it," rang in my head.

"I knew we could count on you to do the decent thing," said Pa. "Maybe, then, we can really call this God's country."

The throbbing in my ears was so loud I could hardly hear when Pa spoke again.

"We'll hope to see you Christmas night, then," Pa said.

I thought I was going to choke. My breath felt cut off. Was Pa talking to a Klan member? He was calling somebody in South Carolina.

"It'll be a nice Christmas present," Pa told the party at the other end of the line.

I couldn't stand to hear another word. Pa was saying exactly the same things I'd heard Mr. Bud and Brother Jake say when we were hiding on the woods road. That tarot card I drew must have been upside down. While Pa was still on the phone I quietly eased to the front door, opened it and slipped out onto the porch.

The bright sun danced around Ma's camellia bushes that bordered the porch. They were loaded with red and pink and white blossoms. It felt all wrong; it didn't fit. It should have been dark and stormy and cold with the creamy camellias burned brown around the edges.

I ran with my terrible thoughts toward the tram road. For the first time in my life the tram failed me. My legs felt as heavy as lead and I had to drag myself along the roadbed. Finally I reached the creek. Should I cross and go to Little Hattie? No. No, I couldn't tell anybody that maybe Pa was a secret Klanner. Not even Little Hattie. I sat on the creek bank and stared into the black velvety water. Just sat there, not really even thinking. It was more like giving up to it, like drowning in that soft, still, dark water.

I don't know how long I had been sitting there when a sudden splash in the water snapped me out of the daze.

I lifted my head and there was Liam standing on the opposite bank. He was grinning and plunking small pebbles into the water.

"Something have you hypnotized?" he asked cheerfully.

"Leave me alone," I muttered.

"You must have been hypnotized," continued Liam. "It took a dozen pebbles to bring you around."

Now that he was being friendly with me, I didn't want to be friendly with him. I had other things on my mind. Besides I didn't like to have anybody hanging around when I was feeling this way.

"I hate people who go around spying," I shouted at him.

"That makes us even," countered Liam. "You owe me one for spying on our camp."

"What are you doing here anyway?" I asked.

"Gathering greens for our mummers' play," he answered.

Then I noticed on the ground beside him a basket stuffed with holly and smilax vines.

"Mummers' Play? What's that?"

"Oh, it's something we do every Christmas. When I was younger we used to put on the mummers' play for people all through the twelve days of Christmas. We made a lot of money, passing the hat, back then. Now we just do it for ourselves."

"Why'd you quit doing it for money?" I asked.

"Trouble from outsiders. Like I said, you can't trust them."

Liam picked up his basket of holly and greens and ran deftly across one of the slick crossties to my side of the creek. I had to admire how good he was on the crossties. Better than me and Kitty and Scrap.

"You know, Missionary Baptist boy," said Liam, "I think I'd like to have you as a friend. But I've been burned, kid. Aye, I've been burned. You'd have to do something to prove to me that you're worth having as a friend."

Again, I was torn between liking him and wanting to shove him into the creek.

"Well, first you'd better learn my name. It's Harrison, not Missionary Baptist boy."

I thought he'd be mad at me but he laughed and slapped his thigh. "That's a beginning," he cried. "Good-bye thieving Catholic gypsy boy and so-long Missionary Baptist boy. Hello, Harrison!"

He punched me lightly on the shoulder.

I stood up and said, "Hello, Liam," and stuck out my hand. Then he backed off a couple of steps and said, "Just hold it right there. That doesn't mean we're any kind of buddy-buddies. You've got to prove it to me, kid."

Then he snatched up his basket of greens for the mummers' play and hightailed it through the woods.

I sat back down and hunched against my knees and stared into the dark waters of the creek.

Night was coming on before I got back to the house.

Aunt Het called, "Get on in here, Harrison, we's waiting supper for you."

Ma, Pa, and Grandma were already at the table, and Pa said grace as soon as I plopped down. It was hard to believe, they all looked so cheerful, especially Pa.

"You're mighty quiet tonight," said Grandma.

It's funny, but Grandma can sniff out quicker than anyone when there's something wrong with me. It's hard to hide anything from her.

"And you're not eating," she added. "You look flushed, child. Let me lay a hand on your forehead."

She came over and pressed her palm to my forehead.

"Well, I'm sure glad I caught this in time. Young man, you're about to come down with a cold. And we're not having any of that right on the verge of Christmas."

"Het!" she called, "boil me a kettle of water and get out some Saint John's herb."

Ordinarily, I'd fight taking the bitter St. John's tea, but I didn't feel like it tonight. And I knew Grandma would insist that I go straight to bed as soon as I drank it. That would be better than sitting through a miserable evening with Pa.

I was sweating under the three quilts Grandma had tucked around me. That's what you're supposed to do when you're full of St. John's tea. I wondered how Kitty Fisher and Scrap were feeling. Were they worried sick about what might happen to them or their pa if the Klan moved in? Could they suspect *my* pa might be a secret Klansman? My forehead burned and my head ached. Finally I dozed off to sleep.

MATTIE DAVIS

THE NEXT MORNING I WOKE UP FEELING drained, but peaceful. A lot of my worries must have sweated out with the St. John's tea. I lay in the warm bed and enjoyed the smell of cured sausages being fried. For a few moments I convinced myself that the terrible thing I'd thought about Pa was a nightmare. Now daybreak was here and it was gone.

The telephone rang—short, short, long; a snappy ring that meant it was the central operator calling, not somebody on our party line. The sound of the ringing cut through my stomach with a knifing fear. I bolted out of bed and started pulling on my clothes.

"It's for you, Mr. Hawkins," called Aunt Het to Pa.

Then she ambled toward my room calling, "Harrison, you coming to breakfast this morning? The grits are getting cold. I can't get this family together this morning!"

"I'm coming," I yelled back.

By the time I had my shoes on and made it to the kitchen, Pa was finished with the call and back at the table.

"Feeling better?" he asked.

"Okay," I said.

"Think you're up to a little trip into town?"

"Sure," I answered.

"Soon as you finish your breakfast, we'll be taking off," Pa said, wiping his mouth and rising from the table.

I rushed through Aunt Het's grits and sausages and soft scrambled eggs and hurried to find Pa. He was loading a big sack of pecans into the back of the pickup truck.

"Mr. Nobie Thompson said he could use some more pecans. His Christmas customers have about wiped him out. Offered ten cents a pound. That's two cents better than a week ago."

Pa seemed pleased about the pecans. I couldn't

figure Pa out. He had looked so worried and had been so sharp with me about the gypsies and the Klan business until he got that telephone call from South Carolina. Ever since then Pa had been smiling and acting friendly and I'd been feeling terrible. Maybe I was wrong. Maybe I had made the whole thing up in my own head. That must be it. But why was I feeling so trembly inside?

"Come on, hop in!" called Pa climbing into the truck cab.

I took a deep breath and felt better and climbed in beside him.

As soon as we were on the road Pa started singing:

> *"Alice, where are you going?*
> *Downstairs to take a bath.*
> *Alice had a figure like a toothpick*
> *And her head was like a tack."*

It was one of my favorite funny-songs that Pa and I often sang together. It was the kind we sang when Ma and Grandma weren't around. So when he clapped me on the knee I joined him in the next line. It was all "da's" and we harmonized on it:

"Da. Da. Da-da-da-da-da."

Pa started the second verse:

"Alice stepped in the bathtub"

Then he gave me the high sign and I sang the next line:

"She pulled out the plug."

Pa sang:

"Oh my goodness. Oh my soul,"

I sang:

"There goes Alice down the hole."

We sang together:

"Oh, Alice where have you gone at?"

Then we harmonized long and slow like old-time barbershop singing on the last line:

"Downstairs to get a bar of soap."

We both broke into laughter. That crazy song does it to us everytime.

We went through a couple of our other favorites and ended up singing "John Jacob Jingle Hammerschmidt." But the trouble with that song is that you can't stop it; it just goes on forever. So we sang it right into the edge of town.

"I'm winded," cried Pa.

"Me, too!" I gasped. But I felt so good after the singing.

"First stop, Thompson's Feed and Fertilizer and General Merchandise!" shouted Pa as we pulled up in front of the big brick store.

Mr. Thompson's place looked like it had more things outside under the tin shelter that fronted the store than it had on the inside. Sacks of feed and fertilizer, tin buckets and mule collars, kegs of nails, boxes of nuts and apples and dried raisins were keeping company with hoes and rakes and axes and pitchforks. It was a wonderful jumble of anything you might ever need on a farm. And it smelled delicious.

I helped Pa get the bag of pecans out of the truck and we pushed our way through the general merchandise to the inside of the store.

"Glad to see you, Mr. Hawkins," boomed Mr. Thompson. "Don't have a pecan left, and customers waiting."

Mr. Thompson didn't waste any time weighing up the pecans and paying Pa. He had customers waiting.

Back in the truck Pa announced the next stop. "Shulkens Hardware, stop number two!" he called out.

We pulled up in front of the hardware store and I hopped out. Pa dug in his pocket and came up with a nickel.

"Here," he said flipping it to me. "You run down the street to Hill's Ice Cream Parlor and get yourself a treat while I do a little trading with Mr. Shulken."

I squeezed my nickel and headed toward Hill's. By the time I got there I had made a decision. I wouldn't buy an ice cream cone. I'd get a tall cup of orange ice with a little silver-looking tin spoon to eat it. Aunt Het and Grandma made ice cream just as good as Mr. Hill's, but they didn't know how to make orange ice. Orange ice tasted good and it lasted a lot longer than ice cream.

When I got back from Hill's Pa was putting a paper bag into the truck.

"I'll just rest this on the floor here," he said, slipping the bag over to my side.

"It won't be in the way of your feet, will it?" he asked.

"No, it's fine," I replied.

I could tell the bag was heavy the way he lifted it.

"One more stop," Pa announced.

But he didn't say what the stop was. I didn't think anything about that until we were passing the last store in town.

"Where's our last stop?" I asked.

"You'll see," Pa answered. He leaned forward and peered at the clouds through the windshield. "Looks like we're going to get some rain."

We drove out past all the houses that surrounded the town, nearly to the edge of the Green Swamp. Suddenly Pa jammed on the brakes, almost bashing both of us into the windshield.

"Whoa, Lizzie!" he shouted to the truck. "Almost missed our turnoff."

He made a sharp turn and steered the truck down a dirt road. The sun pulled behind a cloud and everything took on a gray look. Pretty soon we pulled up under a grove of large live oaks draped in Spanish moss. Half hidden in the moss-covered trees was a big two-story house with porches rambling all around it. A big electric sign was hanging over the front steps. It flashed the word EATS on and off. First EATS came on in yellow, then it flashed blue.

"What is this place?" I asked.

"Mattie Davis's place," answered Pa.

"What're we doing stopping here, Pa?"

"Thought I might pick up a little barbecue, surprise your Ma. Mat makes the best in the county."

Pa got out of the truck and I started to follow him. But he turned around and said, "Stay in the truck and wait for me, Harrison."

He had that worried look on his face again. I watched him walk under the flashing sign. Pa turned all blue and weird-looking as he disappeared into the big house.

I noticed several cars parked under the live oaks, and I could hear music and laughing coming from Mat's place. But there wasn't a soul outside, other than me.

The wind stirred the moss in the low-branched live oaks. Pa was right, I could smell rain on the way. I felt shivery and started climbing back into the truck. My foot struck the package Pa had picked up at Shulken's hardware store and the bag ripped. When I straightened up the bag I saw what was inside. Gun shells! Pa had a gun and a half a box of gun shells that had lasted for years. Pa never had been a hunter, just didn't care for it. What in the world was he going to do with six whole boxes of gun shells? The wind swished the moss against the top of the truck. The first big raindrops peppered the truck top. I started feeling trembly inside again.

It was raining hard when Pa reappeared on the front porch. A big light-skinned colored woman was with him. Even through the slashing rain I knew it was Mattie Davis. She looked like Mr. Bud Highsmith. That is, she looked like Mr. Bud, if Mr. Bud had ever smiled. She was talking to Pa, using her hands a lot. And Pa was shaking his head.

They kept changing color—blue and yellow, cold blue and sickly yellow. Finally they shook hands and Pa dashed for the car carrying a package.

I opened the door on the driver's side and he jumped in.

"Here, hold this on your lap," he said. "Let's get out of here before this dirt road gets boggy."

We drove through the rain, back to the main highway, and headed home. It was raining so hard Pa could hardly see the road. I don't know whether he was concentrating on the road or thinking about something else, but he was quiet and a long way off again.

Before we got home the rain was so hard Pa had to roll down the window and drive with his head outside to see the road.

Just as we turned into the side road to our farm it slacked up.

"That's the way it is with a violent downpour,"

said Pa. "She comes on fast and furious, and it's over just as quickly."

Then Pa drifted back into his own thoughts. That faraway look came over him and I just sat there with the gun shells bumping against my legs.

When we reached our house, I saw Kitty Fisher and Scrap dashing out of the yard with wet newspapers over their heads.

I rolled the window down and yelled, "Hey Kitty! You all coming by tomorrow?"

They stopped and turned back, peering at me from under the soggy newspapers. "Don't think we be coming," answered Kitty.

I hopped out of the truck. "Why not?" I asked.

"Ma says we got to stick close to the house," said Scrap.

"Why?" I asked.

"You know why," said Kitty.

"But tomorrow's Christmas Eve. I thought . . ." I didn't finish.

They turned, pulled the wet newspapers tighter around their heads, and ran down the muddy road.

Pa walked around to my side of the truck.

"You want me to carry the package?" I asked reaching for the gun shells.

"No!" said Pa. "Don't touch that bag."

Then he said, quietlike, "Take the barbecue in to Aunt Het while it's still hot. I'll be in, in a minute."

Pa picked up the bag of gun shells and went toward the barn.

I scooted into the house shivering from the cold wet rain on the outside and the trembly feeling on the inside.

I dumped the barbecue with Aunt Het and rushed out again. The way Kitty Fisher and Scrap had run out of the yard worried me. Something was wrong. I ran down the muddy road after them.

They were near an old barn, almost to their house, before I caught up.

"Wait, Kitty! Hold on, Scrap!" I called.

They turned back and I dashed up to them out of breath and out of words. Now that we were face to face, I didn't know what to say. They looked at me and waited.

"Let's get under that barn shelter out of the rain," I said.

Under the shelter I still didn't know how to get started so I asked, "What's the matter?"

"Nothing," said Scrap.

Kitty looked down at his muddy shoes.

"Everything's the matter," I blurted. "Everything's crazy. Everybody's scared. What's the matter with everybody?"

"I don't know about everybody, but you right, Harrison. We's scared," said Kitty Fisher.

I didn't need to ask, *Scared of what?* I knew it was the Klan. "But they're coming after the gypsies. They won't bother us," I argued.

"Us don't include colored people," said Kitty. "Maybe they won't bother you, but they gonna do something bad to *us.* Fact is, it won't do you no good to be seen acting so friendly with us."

"Yeah, we be better off sticking to ourselves 'til all this mess blows over," added Scrap. "Mr. Bud Highsmith's got it in for us being friends with you anyhow. Pa says Mr. Bud's a secret Klanner. Pa named a lot more—"

"Hush!" commanded Kitty Fisher.

I felt like I was choking. Could they suspect my pa, too? Kitty and Scrap were my best friends in the whole world, and I knew it and they knew it, and something awful was running in on us, shoving us apart, dividing us up in a way none of us wanted.

"It's not right!" I screamed. "It's not right for gypsies, or colored, or anybody else!"

I felt like I would explode.

"I'm going to warn those gypsies, and I'm going to keep on being your friend, and I don't care what happens!" I shouted, and then I started bawling.

They must have thought I was going crazy right there on the spot. Scrap and Kitty each took me by the arms and walked me back into the cool rain.

"Go on home, Harrison," said Kitty Fisher gently. Then he whispered to me, "If you want me to, I'll go with you to warn the gypsies."

I think that's what he said. I was crying so, it was hard to hear.

DREAM AND DECISION

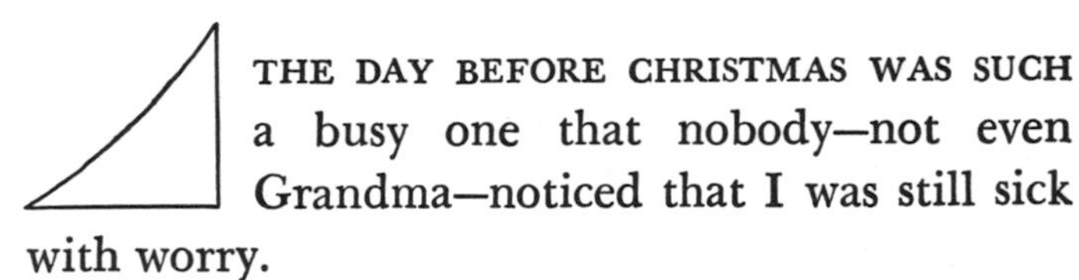

THE DAY BEFORE CHRISTMAS WAS SUCH a busy one that nobody—not even Grandma—noticed that I was still sick with worry.

Aunt Het said to Pa, "I be ready for the big bird now."

She had cooped a large tom turkey for a week and had fed him cracked corn and water. "You got to fatten 'em and clean 'em out if you wants decent eating," Aunt Het explained.

"Harrison, come with me. I need you to help hold the bird," Pa said.

I'm not squeamish about killing chickens or pigs, but I'd never done it to a turkey before. I got the ax while Pa caught the turkey and we met back at the chopping block.

Pa laid the turkey's neck on the block and said, "Hold him right there."

I grabbed hold of the turkey and closed my eyes. A sickening picture burned in my mind. Liam's gashed head looked like the turkey's red coxcomb. I could feel the warm neck throbbing in my hands. I squeezed my eyes tighter to push out the horrible image. Pa sucked in a deep breath and raised the ax. A terrible chill seized me and I trembled all over. The turkey struggled in my hands.

"Huw!" cried Pa as the ax sounded against the chopping block.

I was afraid to open my eyes—scared to death that I'd see Pa standing there in the long white robe of a klansman.

"Harrison!" yelled Pa. "Watch what you're doing. I almost got your hand."

I forced myself to open my eyes.

The turkey lay flopping on the ground with blood spurting from the neck. I felt sick. I couldn't understand why; I'd held many a chicken in the same way, and it never bothered me before.

"You sure you're over that fever you had last night?" asked Pa.

I didn't answer.

"I think you'd better get back to bed," said Pa.

"Tomorrow's the big day. You don't want to be sick on Christmas."

I didn't argue. I needed time to think. I needed time to get past worrying so hard I couldn't think. Going back to bed seemed the best way to get away from everybody. Even if it meant a second dose of St. John's tea.

Ma brought some supper in on a tray. She felt my forehead. "Still a little fever. But you'll be good as new by tomorrow. And you'll know what Santa Claus has left."

I smiled and played along with Ma.

From my room I could hear the radio playing. The news came on. Then, later, *Lum and Abner.* I knew Grandma would go to bed right after *Lum and Abner,* but tonight it sounded as if everyone was stirring around. I realized what they were doing—fixing Santa Claus for me.

After about a half-hour of whispering and tiptoeing about they all went to bed. I lay quiet with my eyes open in the dark. My worry was still there, but I had decided what I was going to do. And I was going to stick to it. Kitty's offer to help made me feel better. But knowing that I'd be going against Pa made my chest ache. Still, it was a relief to have it decided.

I sat on the edge of the bed and waited for a long time. It seemed like hours. I dozed and woke up, startled. Was the phone ringing? Maybe I was dreaming. I dozed again. The sound of a car pulling out of the yard woke me. I pulled the quilt over my head and fell into a deep sleep.

A witch was riding me hard. I couldn't move a muscle in my body, and my breath felt cut off. The dream was a scary one. Scrap and Kitty Fisher and I were running from Mr. Bud Highsmith's dog, who was nipping at our heels. Liam's festered head floated in a field of waving broom sage. Pa's voice saying, "It'll be a nice Christmas present," repeated in my ears like an evil threat. The Chariot card skittered in a whirlwind, first upside down, then right side up, and finally it floated to the ground and fell face down so I couldn't tell which way it was turned. Kathleen Cafferty's long blonde hair floated across the mixed-up scene and fell over my face so thick and heavy I could hardly breathe. If I could just get one toe to wiggle I could break the dream. With a great effort I jerked my knee upwards, and the witch flew off me. I was wide awake, fighting the smothering bedcovers that were all bundled around my head.

I quickly put on all of my clothes except my shoes. Then I crept down the hall and through the living room. The moon cutting through the window splashed on the dark Christmas cedar, making it glow like a silvery ghost tree. It was beautiful and scary.

Sitting on the front steps I put my shoes on. It was time to go, but I held back. I took the time to pick a bunch of snow-white camellias from a bush that grew beside the steps. I wasn't sure who they were for, but I felt better bringing something with me.

My heart was pounding as I left our front yard and headed toward Kitty Fisher's house. I was really scared to go by myself at night to the gypsy camp. I'd feel a lot better if Kitty was with me. *Kitty said he would go,* I kept telling myself. That's what he whispered in my ear. That's what a best friend would do. Wasn't it? When I saw Kitty's house in the moonlight it was all dark, every window of the cabin shuttered tight. I never realized before how small and frail the house looked crouched under a giant water oak. I had the pebble in my hand ready to plunk against the shutter where Kitty slept. But I couldn't throw it. Looking at that little house, I had to tell myself, I had to admit what Kitty and Scrap had tried to tell me. They were colored and I was white, and all the friendship between us didn't make any difference to a lot of people. I couldn't ask Kitty to put himself and his family in danger. It was different for him. We were going to stay friends, I had to hold on to that. But it was never going to be the same. Some mean, scary thing that none of us had ever seen had put a distance between us.

I turned and ran toward the woods road and Broomsage Hollow.

I'd never been on the woods road at night. Patches of speckled moonlight shot through the trees, jabbing at me as I moved along the path. It felt good to run. Gradually the lightness returned to my feet and I ran swift and easy.

The woods road ended abruptly. I pulled up short, panting hard, and blinking my eyes to make sure they weren't playing tricks on me. Broomsage Hollow stretched out toward the creek like a lake of gold, shimmering in the moonlight.

The drab gypsy wagons lining the creek bank were transformed into storybook cottages, twinkling like jewels against the dark creek waters. Ropes of princess pine tied with colored strips of cloth outlined the little houses. Bunches of holly, heavy with red berries, sprouted from the rooftops. And lighted candles flickered in lanterns hung in the Christmas greens decorating the wagons. A big fire blazed in front of the largest wagon where everyone seemed to be gathered. Sitting in the open door of the big wagon I could see the old woman who had the gift of foresight. Didn't *she* know the terrible thing that was about to happen?

I plunged into the golden lake of broom sage and ran toward the magic scene.

THE MUMMERS' PLAY

"I'VE GOT TO TELL THEM. I'VE GOT TO warn them," I kept saying to myself as I pushed through the broom sage.

I intended to rush right into the circle of people gathered around the fire and shout, "The Klan! The Klan! Hitch up your horses and move out of here! The Klan's coming tomorrow and they'll do terrible things to you. Go tonight! I'm your friend. Trust me, and go far away from here!"

But they were all so quiet, staring intently at the old woman sitting in the wagon door. She was singing in a high-pitched, wavery voice. A young man in a suit of many colors stood beside her, plucking a small harp.

Tom Cafferty was the only one who paid any attention to me as I neared the circle. He tipped his cap and motioned me to join the group. They were all concentrated on the old woman. In her quavering voice she sang out:

"I wonder as I wander
Out under the sky
Why Jesus the Savior
Was born for to die?"

I thought I knew all of the Christmas songs there were, but this was a strange one, a sad-sounding one.

The group in front of the old woman sang back the answer to the question of the song:

"For poor lonely people
Like you and like I
Jesus the Savior
Was born for to die."

The old woman finished the song, "I wonder as I *wander,* out under the sky." She held a long time on the high note that fitted the word "wander," then quickly ended the song and dropped her head down on her bosom.

"Now," I thought, "now's the time to shout my warning."

I started to stand up, but the old woman raised

her head and called out in a loud voice, "What news is there?"

No one answered. And for a moment I thought she was calling to me. I stood up and opened my mouth to speak.

Before I could speak she asked again, "What news is there? Tell us, O Morning Cock, what news is there?"

From the top of the wagon where the old woman was sitting there came a crowing sound.

"Cock-a-doodle-doo! Cock-a-doodle-doo!"

And rising out of the bunches of holly that sprouted from the wagon top great wings began to flap. It scared the living daylights out of me, until I saw that it was Liam with colored streamers sewn onto a black coat.

He flapped his arms and crowed a third time, "Cock-a-doodle-doo! Christ is born!" he cried.

Then two young girls dressed all in black rushed up to either side of the old woman. They hovered in front of her, trembling their arms like dark nightbirds.

"When? When is this thing come to pass? Tell us. Tell us, tell the ravens, when is this thing come to pass?" they cried in shivery voices.

Liam, the cock, flapped his many colored wings again and crowed, "This night!"

The old woman moved her hand from her forehead to her heart, then from her right shoulder to her left.

Suddenly a large man jumped up from the circle. He was holding a pair of bull's horns in front of his forehead. Pawing the ground he stamped back and forth in front of the wagon.

"What say you, Ox?" asked the old woman.

"Where is this thing come to pass? Tell the oxen, where?"

"In Bethlehem!" shouted Liam from the rooftop.

A group of children dressed in white rushed to the front of the wagon. They packed close about the old woman with their heads bowed.

"Sheep!" cried the old woman, "have you nothing to say?"

The sheep raised their heads and looked up toward the cock. "Let us go find him," they said all together. Then they asked the cock, "How will we know the way?"

The cock jumped to his feet and pointed into the dark night sky. "Follow the bright star. Follow the Star of Bethlehem!"

"Let us go," shouted Tom Cafferty. "I am the horse," he cried. "Follow me!"

Everyone stood up. Kathleen ran to Tom. I stood up too.

"Let us sing as we go!" cried Liam. "Cock-a-doodle-doo!" he crowed and jumped from the rooftop.

The musician plucked the harp strings and Tom, the horse man, banged a tambourine. With

Kathleen holding his arm he began prancing around the fire. Everyone fell into line behind the horse except the old woman. She started a song:

> *"What child is this who laid to rest*
> *On Mary's lap is sleeping?"*

I knew this song, so I joined in:

> *"Whom angels greet with anthems sweet*
> *While shepherds watch are keeping."*

Liam jumped into the moving procession beside me. He had a strong voice, and we boomed out on the chorus:

> *"This, this is Christ the King,*
> *Whom Shepherds greet and Angels sing,*
> *Haste, haste to bring him laud*
> *The Babe the son of Mary."*

At the end of the chorus Liam said, "How you like slumming with tinkers?"

"Liam, there's something—"

"How'd you like my crowing?" he asked.

"Fine," I said, "but there's something I've got to tell you."

Liam ignored me and asked, "Who are the flowers for?"

I'd forgotten I had brought them. "The old woman," I answered.

"Then give them to her," he said, pushing me out of line toward the wagon.

The old woman was singing with her eyes closed, so I laid the flowers in her lap and ran back to Liam.

"Listen, Liam, everybody here is in danger," I whispered to him.

I don't think he heard me because he kept on singing:

> *"Raise, raise the song on high,*
> *The Virgin sings her lullaby.*
> *Joy, joy for Christ is born,*
> *The Babe, the son of Mary."*

On the second circle around the fire I saw the lights. They were just pale spots in the darkness, but they were evenly spaced like headlights on a car. I pulled out of the circle near the broom sage. Two sets of headlights were moving toward the gypsy camp. Then I could see more—a whole line of them coming from Mr. Bud Highsmith's place.

"No," I thought, "it can't be; not tonight. They're supposed to come tomorrow."

But I knew as sure as life, it was them. I quickly ducked into the nearest clump of broom sage. The circle of people still moved around the fire singing:

> *"So bring him incense, gold and myrrh,*
> *Come peasant, king to own him,*

The King of Kings salvation brings,
Let loving hearts enthrone him."

The old woman pulled herself up in the doorway and pointed with my snow-white flowers to the lights moving toward the camp. She cried out with a loud wail and the flowers tumbled from her hand.

The harp-player's fingers stopped on the strings. The tinkers stood there frozen, the way wild animals do at night when they're caught on the highway in the glare of headlights.

The startled people were quickly surrounded by cars and trucks, and a host of ghostly nightriders burst out at them. I'd always thought of white robes as the clothing of beautiful angels. But these evil figures, with their faces hidden under tall pointed hoods and with blank, black holes for eyes, were the ugliest and scariest things I'd ever seen.

Two of the Klanners ran toward the campfire carrying a long wooden cross. They held it over the fire for a moment and flames burst from its cross-arms. It must have been daubed with tar to catch the way it did. They jammed the pointed end of the cross into the ground and it blazed against the night sky.

The tinkers packed tightly around the large wagon where the old woman sat. Why didn't they run? Or fight? Then I saw several Klanners standing in the back of a pickup truck with guns pointed at the tinkers. It was so deathly quiet you could hear the flames crackling on the burning cross.

The voice of a tall ghost sliced through the silence with razor sharp words. "Bring out the woman and the man!"

From my hiding place in the broom sage I could see that this tall ghost was dressed differently from the others. He had a chain around his neck with a large emblem on it.

"Hear the Imperial Wizard!" shouted another Klansman. "Bring out the woman and her gypsy violator."

Nobody stirred.

The white-robed Klanners with the shotguns jumped down from the truck. They were moving straight toward the clump of broom sage I was hiding behind. I flattened out with my face in the dirt, my heart thumping so loud I was sure they could hear it. Their heavy workshoes plowed into the broom sage. I knew I was lost. They'd see me, or stumble over me.

A foot crushed down on my hand and a pain shot through my arm. I bit my lip and closed my eyes, waiting for the Klanners to discover me.

"Swing over that way," said the Klanner standing almost on top of me. "Close in and cover our boys."

The foot lifted from my hand and the men with the guns moved up to the cowed group of tinkers. I crawled behind a thicker bunch of broom sage a littler further away. My hand was throbbing and I squeezed it hard to cut the pain.

Through the broom sage I could see the night riders pushing their way into the huddled group. Who were they looking for? What did they mean, "The woman and her gypsy violator?"

Their tall pointed hoods bobbed over the heads of the tinkers as the Klanners shoved and pushed them around.

"No! No!" screamed a woman.

I took a chance and stood up to see who was screaming.

At last the tinker men made a move to stop the Klanners. There was scuffling and shouting around the woman.

The nightriders with the shotguns waved them at the tinkers.

"Hold still, you stinking gypsies, or we'll spray you with buckshot!"

A shot sounded and I dropped to the ground again.

Everything was quiet.

I raised myself up enough to peer through the broom sage.

Two nightriders were dragging a woman out of the crowd. I couldn't see her face, but the long yellow hair told me it was Kathleen.

They pulled her toward the burning cross.

Tom Cafferty broke from the group and ran after her.

The Imperial Wizard laughed and cried, "Use the woman for bait; you'll find the man every time. That's the gypsy violator. Take him; he's the thieving Catholic gypsy who dared lure a white woman from her decent, law-abiding family."

Several of the Klanners grabbed Tom. Liam made a move toward his brother, but the harp-player grabbed his hand and held him back. Tom struggled like a wild animal, but there were too many of them. And they overpowered him and dragged him up to the flaming cross. He twisted his head so he could see Kathleen's frightened face. Then he jerked his head back, and such a terrible cry came out of his throat it sent shivers up my back.

I had to do something. I was the only one that wasn't trapped. I'd have to get help. Scrap and Kitty Fisher? No, I couldn't do that to them. Pa? My stomach churned. I'd lost Pa. I wasn't sure I could ever look in his face again. There was nobody. Not a soul. Surely my tarot card was upside down in the deck. I'd just have to hide here in the broom sage and let the nightriders have their way, then help the best I could when they were gone.

The Klanners stripped off Tom's shirt. Then

two of them held his arms. Another one came forward with a bullwhip. He raised his arm and the lash cut a hissing path through the air like an evil snake. With a snap of his wrist it cracked like a pistol shot. My skin crawled.

The bullwhipper looked toward the Imperial Wizard. "Let the violator feel the sting of righteousness!" he shouted.

The leather snake flashed through the air again and this time the crackling sound bit into Tom's flesh. It tore the skin and a red stain spread down his back.

Kathleen screamed.

I couldn't stand it another second. My feet were running. I plunged blindly through the broom sage, putting distance between me and the hell at the gypsy camp. Suddenly, I bumped someone so hard it knocked the breath out of me. We both tumbled into the broom sage.

CIRCLE OF FIRE

KITTY FISHER WAS SHAKING ME.

"Harrison, it's the Klanners?"

"It's them all right, and they're doing terrible things. We've got to stop them, we've got to get help! We've got to stop them. We've got to. . . ."

I couldn't stop saying the same thing over and over.

Finally, I asked, "What are you doing here? It's too dangerous for you here, Kitty!"

"I saw you in our yard," said Kitty.

I could have hugged Kitty when he said that.

"Who? Who? Who? There's got to be somebody," I asked out loud.

Kitty was pulling me away from the horrible scene.

Then it came to me. "I know. Kitty, I know!" I cried.

I grabbed his hand and ran.

The tram road flew by in a blur. After we crossed the creek Kitty knew where we were running. Little Hattie's. It was only a short distance, but my feet seemed to drag as in a nightmare dream. The yellow glow in her window was the friendliest light I've ever seen. It meant she was still up.

I told her as quickly as I could gasp it out what was going on in Broomsage Hollow.

"You two grab a couple of my Christmas brooms," Little Hattie cried, "while I block after the safety matches."

We didn't ask why. We just did what she said. I hoped she could run as fast as we could.

Before we reached Broomsage Hollow we could see the tall fiery cross flickering through the trees. I still didn't know what Little Hattie would do, but I trusted her.

We stopped at the edge of the Hollow and panted for breath. Across the gently waving broom sage we could see the white-robed men still holding Tom Cafferty. They were shaving his head.

The other gypsy tinkers were herded around the big wagon and several nightriders were holding guns on them.

"Fight fire with fire," whispered Little Hattie.

She snatched three of the brooms and lighted them with a match close to the ground where it wouldn't be seen. She handed one to me, one to Kitty, and lit another one for herself.

"Fire the broom sage," she whispered. "We'll start here and block toward the creek in a circle."

I held the burning broom to a clump of sage. Kitty did the same. Fire shot up from the dry stalks and we moved on to the next clumps. Little Hattie scooted from clump to clump. In a couple of minutes our side of the hollow was a fiery lake.

The flames were jumping from one clump of broom sage to another without our having to fire it. A light breeze swept it toward the creek. Soon we had a line of fire moving toward the gypsy camp.

Little Hattie's eyes looked round and wild in the firelight. "Them devils likes to do their dirty work in the dark," she whispered. "We'll put a light on them that'll have half the county blocking here to see what's up."

The nightriders had their backs to our fire, so they didn't see it for a long time. The cowed tinkers saw it, but they didn't let on that anything was happening.

Finally, one of the Klansmen turned and saw our line of fire moving toward them.

"Fire! Fire!" he shouted.

The Imperial Wizard turned and saw the blaze. He raised his arms and called out, "Back to the cars! Get to your cars before the fire cuts us off!"

The white-robed men let Tom and Kathleen go.

"That ought to keep you thieving gypsies in your place for a while!" shouted one of them as he ran towards the cars.

"Hellfire! We was just getting going good," cried another

"Shoot! We ain't even given the niggers a scaring yet!" yelled a tall Klanner.

"Hurry!" commanded the Imperial Wizard. "This blaze can be seen for miles. Get out of here!"

Watching the nightriders through the wall of flames I thought, "This looks just the way our revival preacher described the fires of hell."

Kathleen crumpled and fell to the ground in front of the burning cross. "Oh my God," I gasped, "they've killed her."

I started to move toward the camp.

Little Hattie and Kitty Fisher held me back. "Wait, child. Hold off 'til them devils blocks out," said Little Hattie.

"But Kathleen!" I cried.

"Just probably fainted. That's all. Fainted from relief," reassured Little Hattie.

Tom bent down and scooped Kathleen up in his arms. In the bright light of the burning cross I could see a big ugly cut in his head. Blood streaked down his face.

I strained to go again, but Little Hattie held me fast. "In a minute, child, in a minute."

The minute the nightriders started to flee the tinker men ran to their horses. They led them away from the camp, down the creek a ways, and into the water. All of the women and children followed. Tom carried Kathleen down to the water and several of the women took her from him.

You could hear the nightriders gunning their engines, trying to back up and turn around to get out of the fiery Hollow. The road was a narrow dirt one so they could only snake out one at a time. But they finally all got headed out.

"Now we can block down to the creek," said Little Hattie.

We started moving around the edge of the Hollow, working our way to the tinkers' camp.

"I hope this fire we started don't get out of hand," Kitty said.

"Don't worry, child, the Hollow be a protected place. We used to burn it off every year. Makes the broom sage block back better next season."

Suddenly the line of cars and trucks all stopped. There was more yelling and cursing. Little Hattie and Kitty and I dashed the rest of the way to the camp.

I couldn't figure out what was happening. Gunshots sounded somewhere near the Klan's cars. I couldn't understand why they had stopped. Could they be coming back to finish up what they had started with the tinkers?

Liam and Tom rushed up to me and Kitty and Little Hattie. Liam stopped but Tom brushed past us with a big stick in his hand and started striking the fiery cross. He acted like a wild man, grunting and crying and fighting the burning cross as if it were a living thing. He had a rag tied around his head, but blood still trickled down his face. We stood as if we were hypnotized and watched him destroy the horrible sign left by the Klan.

A truck suddenly roared into the camp and ground to a stop.

"Holy Jesus!" cried Little Hattie. "They's blocking back here. They'll kill us sure! Run!"

Kitty and Little Hattie ran toward the creek.

The bright headlights of the truck shining in my face blinded me. I didn't know which way to run.

The truck door slammed and a man stepped out with a long gun in his hand. I couldn't see his face in the glaring light. I froze and waited to see what the Klansman would do.

"Harrison!" a voice called.

How did he know my name? Could it be Mr Bud Highsmith?

"Harrison!" the man called again.

I recognized the voice. It was Pa—Pa, riding with the Klanners. I wanted to run back into the broom sage, but it was all ablaze.

"Harrison," Pa called again, "run down to the creek and tell the tinkers they can come back. The sheriff and his men have the Klan under control. But we've got plans to make, and we've got to make them fast."

I couldn't move. I didn't understand any of it. Hadn't Pa called the Klan? I'd heard him on the phone calling Latta, South Carolina.

"Don't stand there, Harrison," Pa shouted. "Get everybody up here!"

Liam grabbed me by the hand and pulled me toward the creek.

I was glad to be out of the light, so no one could see me crying. It wasn't straight in my mind yet, but it didn't matter. Pa didn't belong to the Klan. Pa was on the side of the tinkers. That's all that mattered.

When I got back to the camp the place was filled with people. Kitty Fisher's pa was there, and all the colored people who lived nearby. They had seen our fire.

"Can you be packed and ready to travel within an hour?" Pa asked the gypsies.

The tinker men nodded their heads and started hitching up the wagons. Pa told them that his cousin Jonathan in Latta, South Carolina, would give them a safe place for their first camp stop. And, after that, he explained how they had worked it out to send the tinkers from one friend's place to another until they could safely reach their winter home near Pensacola, Florida.

Pa came over and said to me, "I'll be sorry to miss Christmas morning at home this year. But your Ma understands, and I won't rest easy until I get these folks safely to Latta. Cousin Jonathan's going to drive me back tomorrow afternoon."

I just stared at Pa, so relieved I couldn't say a word.

"Don't look so disappointed," said Pa. "I think Santa Claus has already visited our house."

Then Pa asked Kitty Fisher's papa to round up the men and check the fire to make sure it burned out in the Hollow.

Pa stared at the burning broom sage shaking his head. "It must have been the hand of providence that would cause the broom sage to catch fire just in the nick of time," he said.

Little Hattie and Kitty and I looked at each other. She winked.

"The hand of providence blocks in mysterious ways," she said in a solemn voice, looking Pa straight in the eye.

When the wagons were all hitched and ready to go, Tom Cafferty drew Pa aside. They stood talking for a couple of minutes. Then Pa came over to where Little Hattie and I were standing.

"Harrison, you and Little Hattie ride with the Caffertys back to our place. Mrs. Kathleen Cafferty's gone into labor. Bring Aunt Het as soon as you get to the house."

Liam and Tom and I sat on the seat in front of the wagon. Little Hattie climbed inside to be with Kathleen.

At the same time Pa jumped on the front seat of the big wagon that belonged to the old woman with the gift of foresight. The gypsy wagons turned toward the main highway and we drove around the edge of the burning broom sage and headed for home.

Ma and Grandma were up and stirring around the kitchen when we pulled into the back yard. I hopped down from the wagon and rushed in to tell them about the Caffertys.

"You just bring Miss Kathleen into the house and we'll get her into bed," said Ma.

"Thank you, ma'm," said Tom Cafferty, "we'll be just fine in the wagon."

Little Hattie popped out of the wagon door. "Miss Kathleen needs a granny woman, right now. She be blocking close to delivery."

"Go bring Aunt Het," said Grandma.

Little Hattie darted off into the night.

Ma stepped up to the wagon door and looked in

at Kathleen. "Don't you worry now, we'll get you inside the house, and Aunt Het will be here in a few minutes."

"That's mighty kind of you, ma'm," said Kathleen, "but tinker women have their babies in their own houses. They believe it brings good fortune and long life to be born in a traveling house. I'm a tinker woman now and determined to follow tinker ways."

Ma looked puzzled.

"We'd be much obliged if you'd let us drive the wagon into your barn for shelter," said Tom.

Ma still looked a little confused. "Certainly, of course," she replied.

Liam and I ran to open the barn doors.

Ma followed us, still mumbling that the barn just didn't seem the right place to be having a baby.

Grandma looked at her and said, "Leave them be, daughter."

That settled the argument, and Tom Cafferty drove the wagon into our barn.

We all stood around feeling nervous and useless until Little Hattie got back with Aunt Het. Then Aunt Het took over.

"It's high time all of you went to bed and got out of my way," she said. "I don't need no congregation witnessing my granny work."

She took a kettle of hot water off the stove and headed toward the barn.

I was so tired I could hardly wait to get undressed and into bed. I left my socks on and crawled under the covers. I lay there shivering but feeling the warmth of the quilts creep around me. It felt so wonderful to have Pa back. But it felt so rotten and terrible to have doubted him. It was like having fever and chills. Pa could never be perfect for me again, because I'd doubted him in my mind. And I'd found out that there were things that frightened him too. I knew now that being perfect was baby stuff, and I'd outgrown it. I knew I would go on loving Pa, perfect or not. But I was sure glad I hadn't lost him the way I feared I had. And maybe Kitty and I could . . .

Just before I gave up to sleep, a nagging question popped into my head: *How did Pa know the Klan was coming tonight? They were supposed to come on Christmas day. How did he know they were coming early?* It troubled me for a few minutes before sleep overtook me.

SIGN OF THE VEIL

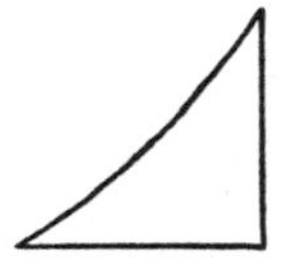

NOBODY WOKE ME. I KNEW IT WAS LATE; the sun was streaming through the windows halfway across the room.

In the kitchen I found Aunt Het, Ma, and Grandma drinking black coffee.

"Well?" I asked.

They all laughed.

"Well, yes," anwered Aunt Het. "There be a new Christmas baby out in the barn."

"Was it a boy?"

"No," said Aunt Het. "It be a girl child. A pretty little girl child."

"Can we see the baby?" I asked.

"I don't think it would be proper to go rushing in on the Caffertys this soon," Ma said.

"Besides," cried Grandma, "you haven't even seen what Santa Claus left last night."

I knew all right, but my mind was so much on Pa and the tinkers I'd forgotten.

We all trooped into the living room and I played along with the Santa Claus business. There was the electric wood-burning set just like I'd asked for. But there was another little box that I hadn't expected.

I tore the wrapping off the surprise package and opened the box lid. Inside was a figure of a sailor with a knapsack on his back. I knew it was a piggy bank as soon as I saw the slot in the sailor's bag.

"Hey, this is really great!" I cried. "I can put all my buffalo nickels in the sailor's bag." I'd been saving them in a cardboard box.

"Shake the bank," said Grandma.

It clinked when I shook it.

I couldn't help saying, "That Santa Claus sure knows a lot about me."

We all laughed.

Aunt Het served a scrape-together dinner in the middle of the day. I experimented with my wood-burning set for a while, then went out to the barn to look for Liam.

The big doors on the front of the barn were closed. I remembered Ma said it wouldn't be right to go intruding on Kathleen and the new baby, so I circled the barn. Out in back, in a sunny spot where there was a pile of logs, I came upon Liam. He was busy whittling on a piece of wood and didn't see me until I was right on him. I must have scared him because he jumped when he saw me.

"Holy Christ!" he said. "It's you! I'm still jumpy from last night."

"Mind if I sit?"

"Nay, sit if you like."

I climbed onto the pile of logs and sat down beside him. Then I saw what he was whittling.

"That's really something," I said, admiring the finely carved horse he was putting some finishing touches on.

"A little something I learned, to make a few pennies."

"A thing as pretty as that ought to bring right much," I said.

"Not much," he replied. "Folks expects to get things cheap from the likes of us."

"How much would you want for the horse?" I asked, counting in my head the nickels I had in my sailor bank.

Liam didn't answer for a while. He rubbed his finger over the horse's mane and then carved a few little strokes. As I watched him I wanted to have that horse. It seemed like owning it would be like having a magic charm. Our lives had crossed and we'd probably never see each other again, but the horse would link us and bring us luck. I'd never believed in good luck charms and stuff like that. But this horse was different.

"I'd be interested in buying the horse, if it didn't cost too much."

Liam rubbed the carving with the palm of his hand. But he still didn't say anything. After a good long while of just sitting there and rubbing the horse he finally turned to me.

"Here," he said, shoving the horse in my hands. "It's yours. It's payment for what you did for us last night."

I pushed the horse back into his hands. "You don't owe me for that!" I was getting mad at him. How much did he expect me to do to prove I wanted to be his friend?

"Aye, you're right," he said with a smile. "That was mean of me. I just hate to be beholden to anybody."

Then Liam laid the horse in my lap. I didn't touch it.

"It's a gift," he said. "A gift of friendship."

I picked it up and jumped off the log pile. "Race you to the cow pasture and back!" I yelled.

Liam sprinted off the logs and tore after me.

* * *

Pa and Cousin Jonathan finally got home about four o'clock. Aunt Het and Grandma started fixing our big Christmas meal.

I was itching to ask Pa how he found out the Klanners were coming early. But Cousin Jonathan never stopped talking for a second and I couldn't get my question in edgewise. Besides, it was something I wanted to ask Pa privately.

My chance came when Pa went to the barn to tell Tom Cafferty that the tinkers were safely on their way. I followed him.

"Pa, I've got to ask you something."

"Yes?" asked Pa.

There was no way to beat around the bush. "Pa, how did you know the Klanners were coming last night?"

"I'll trade you an answer for an answer," said Pa. "You tell me how you happened to be in the tinker camp last night and I'll tell you how I knew about the Klan."

"I asked first, Pa."

"Fair enough. Mattie Davis called me last night. Mat's got all kinds of connections, and she got word the Klanners had changed plans and were coming early. Hardly gave me time to get in touch with the sheriff. I had to drive to town and wake him up in the middle of the night. The tinkers will never know about Mat's Christmas gift to them. And for that matter no one else around here is to know. Not a soul, Harrison."

Pa was trusting me with grown-up secrets. I felt so guilty about mistrusting him, and so good at the same time . . . I wanted to let Pa know how I felt, but I couldn't put it in words. So I said, "I'm glad the sheriff put them all in jail."

"They're not in jail, Harrison. The sheriff and his men roughed up a few of them and chased them over the border."

"But what about Mr. Bud Highsmith and his friends from around here?"

"Everybody looks the same under a Klan robe. They all crossed over into South Carolina. The sheriff has done his duty, and his authority very conveniently ends at the border."

"Pa, will the Klan come back again?"

"Probably."

"Do you think they'd hurt Kitty Fisher and Scrap?"

"Their skin's the right color."

"Why, Pa, why?"

"That's a hard one, Harrison. And there's no simple answer. I've pondered it myself and it's something I'm not sure I can make clear to you. A part of it's fear—those high and mighty night-riders are for the most part scared little men hiding under bedsheets who need to have somebody they can bully and look down on. I reckon people have been frightened of things that are different since the beginning of time. It can be different color of skin, a different religion, or even different languages and customs. Do you understand what I'm getting at?"

"I'm not sure," I answered.

"Your Grandma would tell you that they're just poor white trash and that quality folks would never resort to such meanness. . . . But there's more to it than that. There's something in all of us that wants to be top dog, that wants to keep *our kind* in control. Human decency doesn't seem to be a God-given gift. It's a precious thing you have to learn early and keep working at."

Pa had never talked to me like this. I was so full, I thought I'd choke.

"Now you've gotten me off the track, young man, and you haven't given me an answer for an answer yet."

I was planning to only tell Pa that I had sneaked out to warn the tinkers and stumbled into their mummers' play, but now I wanted to tell him about Little Hattie and the fire and everything.

"Liam told me they were going to do a mummers' play," I started to explain. I really intended to tell him the rest, even how I was afraid he might be in with the Klan, but Cousin Jonathan came up and joined us and the chance was gone forever.

After dinner Pa asked Ma to fix a Christmas meal for the Caffertys.

"The baby's practically a day old," said Pa. "I don't see why we can't make a social call and bring a little gift of dinner."

Ma said, "Making a social call out in our barn seems a little odd. But I'm eager to see that new baby."

It was just first dark when we left the house with a big basket of turkey, ham and dressing, and pie. Grandma and Aunt Het put on fresh aprons and their Sunday hats for the occasion.

At the last minute I had the strongest wish to bring something of my own to give the Caffertys' new baby. I rushed back and grabbed the fruit-cake Grandma had made for me.

"No," I thought, "Grandma might be hurt if I gave away her gift without asking. Besides the baby can't eat fruitcake anyway. I'll have to bring something that's really mine."

My eyes lighted on the little sailor piggy bank. That was it!

When we got to the barn I was surprised to see Scrap and Kitty Fisher and Little Hattie standing out front. The barn door stood partly open.

Little Hattie had her tow sack with only one broom left in it.

At the barn door Pa called out, "Anybody home?"

Inside, Liam stepped from behind the wagon and said, "Aye, we are all here."

"Is Mrs. Kathleen Cafferty up to seeing a few folks?" Pa asked.

"I'll ask, sir," said Liam.

He disappeared inside the wagon.

In a couple of minutes Liam came out and propped the wagon door open. A lantern hanging from the ceiling lighted the inside of the little house with a warm, mellow glow. Kathleen was sitting up in bed with the baby in her arms. She looked tired and pretty and happy all at the same time.

Tom Cafferty stepped out. He moved stiff like his back was hurting, but he managed a big smile and said, "Welcome to our house."

Pa tipped his hat to Kathleen and said, "It's a pleasure to see everything turned out all right, ma'm."

All of the women crowded into the wagon. After carrying on about the new baby, Ma put the basket on a chest by the foot of the bed. "Some Christmas cheer," she said to Miss Kathleen.

"I thank you, but you shouldn't—"

"It's just a little nothing for the Christmas baby," said Grandma, making light of the big basket of food.

Aunt Het checked the baby and fussed around with the bed clothes.

Finally they came out and Scrap and Kitty Fisher and I went in. The baby was asleep but I could see dark curly ringlets sticking out from the cap on her head. She was kind of red and wrinkled and looked a lot like the old lady with the gift of foresight.

Scrap reached into her pocket and pulled out a strange-looking necklace. It was made of pieces of root strung on a red string.

"Me and Kitty brought the baby a Jerusalem root necklace," she said, handing it to Kathleen.

"That's very kind. Did you make it yourself?"

"Yes," said Scrap. "Kitty dug up the roots and I strung it. It be good to keep the baby from having croup."

"Thank you," said Kathleen. "The necklace is a wonderful gift."

I couldn't think of anything special to say so I held out my sailor bank and said, "Something for the baby, Merry Christmas."

"Thank you and Merry Christmas," said Kathleen. "Your gift will be a reminder of the kind strangers I've met in my travels."

We stood around in the barn and talked with the Caffertys for a good while. Pa and Cousin Jonathan made plans for the Caffertys to follow in a few days the same route the other tinkers had taken. Before Kitty Fisher and Scrap left they promised we'd get together the next day.

I pulled Liam aside and asked him, "Will you show me some more with the tarot cards tomorrow?"

He looked sharply at me and said, "You trying to learn the secrets of the traveling people? I thought you didn't believe in stuff like that."

"Tomorrow, Liam?"

He smiled. "Tomorrow."

By the time we left the barn the stars were out. I followed behind Aunt Het and Grandma toward the house.

"Baby looks fine," said Aunt Het. "I was a might worried. Never delivered one with a caul over the face before."

"What's a caul?" I asked. "The baby's all right, isn't she?"

"Baby's fine," said Aunt Het. "A caul be just a little thin skin over the face, like a veil. I've heard of it all my life, but this be the first one I've ever delivered."

The old gypsy woman's words came back to me—*I'm waiting for a child born under the sign of the veil.*

Pa said, "I'm ready for some coconut pie now."

"Me too," said Cousin Jonathan. "I couldn't make it to dessert after such a big dinner."

I looked up at the night sky so bright with stars, and suddenly one of them streaked across the heavens.

"Make a wish," cried Aunt Het, pointing to the falling star.

We all stood still for a moment.

For the first time in my life I couldn't think of anything to wish for. There was nothing I needed or wanted right now. Watching the star sweep across the sky, all I could feel was relief washing my worries and fears away. I let the glimmering sign pass without a wish. Then I whispered to the sparkling Christmas sky, "Thank you."

Author's note

CIRCLE OF FIRE is rooted in the rich, black soil of the coastal Carolinas, where during the late 1930's rural life had a special glow. This section weathered the Great Depression better than most; the soil never turned to dust, choking instead of feeding, as so much of the southwest did. Although there was little hard cash around, the land remained bountiful. And if you were a farm child growing up during those years, you might well have been unaware that they were years of poverty. Everything seemed secure On the surface there was great tranquility—as long as everyone kept to what was considered "his rightful place."

It was also a time when language was used in a different way; "colored" was the respectable term used by both whites and blacks. Bigots used either "nigger" or "nigra," both equally offensive. Most children under twelve, black or white, found no need for any terminology; they simply called each other by first names or nicknames.

The North/South route is still used today by many gypsies, though second-hand Cadillacs have replaced horse-drawn vehicles. Middle European gypsies predominate now, but a few Irish tinker groups still make the trek. The gypsy legend about the nails used to pin Christ to the cross comes from the oral tradition of the Irish tinkers. The Ku Klux Klan grows and expands, reaching even into the alien territory of the North. *Circle of Fire,* set in the 1930's, is about the turbulent drama that occurred when someone dared step outside that "rightful place." These same events could happen today.